They Think I Invented Pizza

Josh Walker

Look for more books
by Josh Walker:

Luke Coles and the Flower of Chiloe
Luke Coles and the Forest Assassin
Luke Coles and the Curse of Corpo Seco
Luke Coles and the Army of Cesares
Luke Coles Anthology
Caleuche Chronicles
Phoenix Dawn and the Rise of the Witch
Shadowed Dreams
Delivered: True Stories in Pizza Delivery
Monster Attack
Forgotten Places Anthology
Mission Memories
They Think I Invented Pizza 2: Dungeon Pixies

They Think I Invented Pizza

Printed in the U.S.A. and Great Britain

1st edition

For more information see
www.facebook.com/joshwalkerbooks
or
www.joshwalker.fun

ISBN: 978-1-944621-28-5

Library of Congress Control Number: 2021915578

Pete is a college student and pizza delivery driver. When he finds himself in a new world, he must discover how his skills will make him the hero that saves his new world.
PIZZA
PIZZA
PIZZA

Zoey is Pete's best friend and fellow delivery driver. Like Pete, she finds herself in Round. And Round has changed her in a way that no one expected.
PIZZA

Josh Walker

Dedicated to my amazing daughter Esperanza, one of the kindest, most creative, and inspiring people I've ever known

Josh Walker

12

Acknowledgements

A huge thank you to all the amazing BETA readers that helped me with reviewing this book. Their feedback made this one of the most fun stories—for me as an author anyway—that I've been able to tell. As such, I want to give a personal shoutout to each of them. Thank you Shandy Star Mager, Diego Chavez, and Kaleb for your honest critiques and suggestions. Thank you to Gabe Howe, Lex Steeleman, Aidan Smith, and Liiam Steelman for the encouragement. Due to feedback like yours, I fully intend to continue the adventures of Pete the pizzaman in future books. Thank you to Kai and Niko; I promise to add more about Zoey's backstory and about her pizza peel in future books. Thank you to my nieces: Becca, Katie, and Karissa, and my nephew Justin. They've supported my books from the beginning and always have great ideas about where my characters should go. In the foreword, I will explain the contributions my daughter, Esperanza, gave in helping me finish this book, but I wanted to thank her here. Finally, thank you to all the returning readers. Your support has always been and will continue to be the reason why I write.

Josh Walker

Foreword

8/4/2021

My daughter's favorite shows are anime, and her favorite books are light novels and manga. Specifically, she enjoys isekai, a subgenre of the manga/anime/light novel culture.

In isekais, the main character finds themselves in a different world, be it by reincarnation or by teleportation. Usually, the protagonist has some spirit guide that brings them to the new world, and often times, that world runs on video game or board game mechanics. If you enjoy this book and want to look into some anime that falls in the same genre, here is a list of what my daughter watches: *Rising of the Shield Hero*, *That Time I Got Reincarnated as a Slime*, *So I'm a Spider so What*, *Didn't I say to Make My Abilities Average in the Next Life*, and *Kuma-Kuma Bear*.

As I watched these shows with her, I was writing <u>Delivered: True Stories in Pizza Delivery</u>, and a pizza themed isekai began to form in my head, but I wasn't set on writing it until one day when my daughter came home from school. She explained to me that the librarian at her school said my books were too big to be in an elementary school library, and she begged me to write something that *could* go in her school's library.

The next day, while she was at school, I wrote out the first two chapters to this book. When she came home, we read them together, talked about them, and discussed where she wanted the story to go. At this point, she began to draw sketches of the characters and give them names, including this book's villain. On page 198, I included a drawing of said villain done from her original pencil work.

When my daughter left for school the next day, I outlined the book in full and set a goal of doing one to two chapters a day. Each day when she returned home, the first thing she wanted to do was read those chapters with me, providing me plenty of motivation to keep to my writing goal. As we read together, I did my first round of edits and incorporated her notes for further chapters. Over the next three weeks, I wrote the rough draft of this book and edited the second draft.

After we finished the second draft, I rushed to finish four more drafts, running the manuscript through different types of editing software. Exactly one month after I began writing, I finished my sixth draft and sent the book to the amazing BETA reader volunteers I mentioned in the acknowledgements, and we began to commission artwork based on my daughter's drawings. I should note that at some point during the book's creation, my daughter and wife did the uniform designs for the pixies, Pete, and Zoey, so the artists had plenty of concept drawings from which to draw inspiration.

The cover artist—Manuel Aguila—had done all four of my Luke Coles covers and it was great to work with him again. He always seems able to read my mind and draw exactly what I am thinking.

In the end, many creative people, test readers,

and editors helped to create this work. The most important of those—to me—was my daughter. I'm proud and excited to share this story that she and I created together.

Welcome to the world of Round.

Josh Walker

1: No One is Home

Everyone loves pizza, Pete the pizzaman more than most. So he sighed at the situation in which he found himself. It would be his last delivery of the night, three large pies, two pepperoni, one cheese.

The home had been easy enough to find. A green porchlight matched the delivery instructions, and at midnight, no other houses had their lights on. On that porch, he stood, waiting for someone...anyone...to answer the door.

Should I knock again? He wondered. *Yup, I need to knock again.* Knock. Knock. Knock. He would have rung the doorbell, but the house didn't have one. Instead, the place where a doorbell used to be boasted a small hole. Exposed wires poked out. The paint on the wires matched the siding.

Should I call them? His eyes glanced at the customer's phone number on the top of the credit card receipt. Then he dropped the receipt on his pizza bag, and he used the same left hand to fish out a phone from his pocket.

It was a windless night, a rare occurrence in Cheyenne, Wyoming. Something about it didn't seem right. Even so, he didn't need to worry about the receipt blowing away, so he wasn't going to complain. He looked at the phone number by the customer's name and called.

No one answered.

Three pizzas aren't that heavy, not under normal circumstances... But after two minutes of standing there, they'd begun to weigh on his right bicep. He knew he wouldn't be able to stay there much longer.

I should get them back to the car. I'm wasting time. And time wasn't something he had that night. If he could get dishes done before 2:00 AM, he'd be able to watch when the new episode of his favorite isekai premiered.

Isekais were some of his favorite stories. They involve someone who goes to a new world, sometimes by dying and reincarnating, sometimes by teleporting, sometimes by both. In the new world, they live a new life full of adventure. Why couldn't something cool like that happen to him?

Tired steps carried him back to the car. Once there, he placed the pizza bag on the passenger seat. At the same time, he sat in his own seat.

I'll text them and wait five minutes before I leave. He lifted his phone and snapped a picture of the porch, sending it to the number with a message:

This is Pete the pizzaman. I'm here with your food. If no one comes to get it within the next five minutes, I'll have to take it back to the store.

He wouldn't mind if he had to take it back to the store with him. Whenever that happened, the manager canceled the order in the computer system. Then the employees got to eat the pizza... And if there was something Pete liked as much as isekai, it was pizza.

Some of his co-workers weren't as excited about pizza. They'd eaten so much of it that they'd grown tired of it. One had gone as far as to say, "pizza turns to ash in my mouth."

Pete wondered why he hadn't grown tired of it. He supposed it had to do with his childhood. On Monday night, his family would gather, and they'd make pizza.

His dad would handle the dough prep. One by one, he'd take turns with each of the siblings. He taught them how to toss the dough, how to make sauce from scratch. Pete's mother would prepare the cheese and toppings. Each topping got its own small plate on the dining room table.

A smile snuck across Pete's face. Those were some of his favorite memories. He had a healthy, loving relationship with his parents and with his siblings. Even so, those Mondays didn't happen anymore. His brothers and sisters were too busy with work, college, and social endeavors. He was occupied with those things, too: balancing work, video games, and school.

He glanced at the clock. Since he'd sent the text, five minutes had come and gone. It was time to head back to the store.

After he put his key in the ignition, he turned it, and the engine roared to life. He tapped a button on the steering wheel, and a woman's voice spoke. "Please, say a command."

"Call," he began, reading the number off the receipt.

It went straight to voicemail.

"This is Pete the pizzaman. Since no one seems to be here, I'm taking your food back to the store. If you call us soon enough, we will be able to bring it back. If not, we'll refund your credit card. I hope you have a great night." As he finished the last word, he clicked a different button on his steering wheel, and his phone hung up.

Then he began to drive back to the store, moving with a slow caution through the neighborhood streets before reaching one of the avenues.

He hit the call button on the steering wheel again. When the woman's voice asked for a command, he answered. "Call Zoey."

"Calling Zoey on cell." He could hear a few clicks and the faint echo of a dial tone. Then it rang.

Halfway through the first ring, Zoey answered. "What's up?"

"They didn't answer the door, didn't answer their phone. I sent them a text with a picture of their house." Pete slowed to a stop at a red light.

"If they call back, I'll let them know." She hung up.

He noticed some movement in the bushes to the right. When he cast his gaze in that direction, he saw a raccoon. It sent a chill down his spine.

Trash pandas might look cute, but he knew better than to trust the tenacious creatures. One time, one had snuck in his car through an open window. It was trying to pull the hot bag through the window when he intervened. Instead of running off, it went on the offensive. In the end, Pete ran.

The light turned green, and Pete continued unabated the rest of the way back to the store. He parked behind it, got out of his car—he brought the undelivered pizzas with him—and made his way inside.

When Zoey saw him, she smiled. Her bright white teeth contrasted against dark lipstick. She had her black hair cut at shoulder length. It was smooth and shiny with dyed red tips. "At least you'll have some pizza for when you watch your show tonight." Then her lips turned down at the corners, an eyebrow raised, and her voice took on a more serious tone. "Unless they ordered something gross?"

"Pepperoni and cheese." He answered, slipping past her. In case the customer called back, he left the order on the heat racks.

He was in such a hurry that he didn't notice her following behind him. As such, when he spun to head back to the dish pit, he almost ran into her. "Sorry about that."

"No worries." She flicked his hat. You'll owe me for that later, though."

"Yeah?" He shied back, her piercing emerald eyes staring at him.

"Yeah," she stepped forward, poking him in the chest with her index finger. "You'll have to share some of your pizza with me. And tomorrow when we play, you'll owe me one of your drops. Nothing big, a potion or something."

"Right," he relaxed. Though, he wasn't sure what he was afraid of. He liked Zoey a lot. She was funny, liked the same shows, did the same job, had a great sense of humor, and was gorgeous. What was the worst that she would do to him? Make him go on a date with her? Would she? That would be awesome. He went back to being nervous again. "Uh... Pizza...share...sure thing." After an awkward few seconds of silence, he asked. "How much work do you have left to clean up front?"

"I'll finish before you do." She winked.

"We'll see about that."

An hour later, Pete was on the way home, excited he'd make it in time for his show. Driving at night was easier for him than driving in the day. He loved the empty roads... To be specific, he loved not having to worry about other drivers.

Of course, that didn't mean he didn't come across obstacles. Two blocks away from his house—for example—while on a residential street, a cat ran across the middle of the road. It crossed straight in front of him.

His brain took a second to react to the animal. If not for the single white spot on the center of its forehead, he doubted he would have seen it at all. When his brain did catch up, it shouted, 'a cat, oh, gosh, it's a cat. CAT!'

He slammed his right foot on the pedal, the tires screeched, and he came to a stop. The animal froze in place, inches away from his bumper. Then it sped the rest of the way across the street.

A woman with chestnut hair chased behind it. He hadn't noticed her before. At first glance, he guessed she was older than him. Even so, she couldn't have been over thirty. He kept his eyes on the woman and cat as they reached a tree, and the cat sped up it.

Pete contemplated helping them; he had the time. Part of him felt obligated to help. If he didn't stop, and something happened to the woman, and he read about it the next day on a local online news page…well, he couldn't let it get to that point. He understood he was dramatic. In the end, it wouldn't take him long to climb a tree and grab the cat.

Without further hesitation, he pulled next to a curb: parking his vehicle, shutting off the engine, hopping out, and walking toward the tree.

The girl stood at the bottom, speaking with soft words to the animal. "Come down, Max. We need to go home."

While still at a distance—he didn't want her to think he was sneaking up on her—Pete spoke. "Do you need some help? I can climb the tree and get him down for you?"

She turned. Where he thought it would surprise her to see him, it didn't. Instead, her tone seemed expectant. It was like she was waiting for him. "If it isn't too much trouble, that would be amazing. Thank you."

"Don't worry," he told her, examining the tree. On the far side, it looked like it would be easier to get up. He looped to that part of the trunk and began to climb. "I'll get your cat for you."

He felt the woman's eyes on him as he climbed. In a way, it made him feel nervous. He hated when people looked at him. If he slipped, or fell, or worse…like tearing his pants on a branch…he didn't want witnesses.

Nervousness aside, at some point, he realized he was well over twenty feet above the ground, on a narrowing branch. He had two feet to go before he reached the cat, solid concrete below him. When he got to that point, fear replaced the nervousness.

One foot to reach the cat.

The cat inched away.
One and a half feet to reach the cat.
Six inches to reach the cat.
He reached for it, and it lunged at his face, swiping at his left cheek. His hand swung up to block, and he lost balance, falling face-first toward the sidewalk.

Josh Walker

2: Pizza and Games

Pete's sense of hearing returned before anything else. When he remembered what had happened, the sounds he heard surprised him. There were no sirens, no rushed voices of emergency medical workers. The woman with the cat didn't ask him if he was okay.

Instead, he heard…was it ski ball? Was it bowling? It seemed more like ski ball. Where both activities involve the sound of a ball rolling across a hard surface, this sound ended in a hollow thud, not with the crash of pins.

Beeps and bops accompanied the sound. It reminded him of video games, but not modern ones. These sounds were from '80s and '90s video games.

He heard kids playing. For how long had he been asleep? If kids were awake, he had to have been out for hours. Was he in the hospital? That might explain some of the electronic sounds. The ski ball sound might be a cart with food on it. But why would they let kids run around, playing in the halls? That didn't make sense. He tried to lift his eyes to see, but his eyelids were heavy.

His sense of touch began to return. Air conditioning pushed down on him from above, giving his arms and shoulders goosebumps. He wondered why he felt the air current so pronounced against his shoulders. At that point, he realized he was in a sitting position, and he was wearing a tank top. Hard plastic supported his back, curving under his legs. It was a booth or a bench, not a chair.

His upper body inclined forward, arms crossed under his head. Was he lying on a table? He tried to open his eyes again. His eyelids remained heavy.

What kind of hospital puts people in tank tops? And what is that smell? It didn't smell like a hospital, nor did it smell like the cool morning air he'd experienced when he was outside during the tree incident. No, this smell was something else, something familiar; it was the smell of pizza.

He could already taste the pepperoni, and that was the last bit of motivation he needed to force his eyes open and take in his surroundings. From his head resting on crossed arms position, neck crooked so he was looking to the side, he took it all in.

What he saw wasn't a hospital. It wasn't emergency crews rushing to help him. It *was* something he hadn't seen in years, not since his childhood. People walked around in gawky animal costumes with gigantic heads. One was a bear. One was a giant mouse. The bear held a microphone. The mouse had a guitar strapped over his shoulder and a cup-shaped hat atop the center of his head. Out of the hat poked a tiny propeller.

They each wore goofy pink and turquoise shirts. The shirts had a Pizza and Games logo embroidered over the left side of their chest.

A non-costumed employee helped customers who sat around a circular, red table. Pete guessed there were more tables, but still unable to move, he could only stare at the one in his line of sight.

On the other side of the table, he saw arcade games, ski ball, and basketball hoops. The hoops were the ones with the ramps under the basket, so the balls return to the shooter after each shot. This version of the machine moved the baskets toward and away from the shooter. Kids occupied all the games, laughing and playing all the while.

"Ugghh…" he grunted as he used his shoulders and arms to push, and he lifted his head up from the table. Joints cracked and popped, but with each passing second, he seemed more awake, more alert. When he gathered enough strength, he lifted his hands over his head, leaned back, and stretched.

"Ah, good, you're awake." The voice was male, and it spoke in a British accent, one of the more proper dialects, one Pete would expect to hear from royalty or nobility.

He moved his eyes in the direction of the sound. When they fell upon the source, they widened, and his heart began to beat heavy.

It came from a cat, sitting across from him at the same table. It wasn't a human in a cat costume like the mouse and bear from before. This was an actual, true to life, talking cat. Its face was that of a cat, anyway, covered in black hair with a familiar white spot on its forehead. In more ways than not, its body and size seemed human, aside from the smooth black fur which coated its arms and shoulders.

Pete assumed the fur-covered the rest of the animal as well. But he couldn't tell for sure...because it wore a bright orange tank top, covering its chest. A print of a lizard wearing sunglasses rested in the center of the tank top.

Pete looked down at his own tank top. They matched. He groaned, embarrassed by the wardrobe. Then he realized things were much worse than the tank top. He wasn't wearing any pants. *This must be a nightmare*, he convinced himself; *I'm still facedown on the concrete. This is all happening in my brain.*

Then he wondered if the cat was wearing pants. Then he realized it didn't matter. "Is this a dream?"

"A dream?" The cat repeated. "It isn't real if that's what you mean?"

"Isn't real?" Pete's confusion grew.

The cat sighed, "let me explain. My name is Max. I have something I need to ask you, a request as it were."

"Max?" Pete remembered the name. "You're the cat in the tree! You scratched my face. You made me fall!"

"Let bygones be bygones," Max yawned. "As far as this place goes…it's an illusion. I wanted you to wake up somewhere where you felt comfortable. If I'm not mistaken, this is such a place?"

Pete glanced. Now that he took the time to look around, to take in everything, he recognized the joint. When he was a kid, his grandfather used to take him to that exact Pizza and Games. They'd go out together on a special day. That's what his grandpa called them. They'd buy a toy at the store. Then they'd end the day at Pizza and Games. "You brought me to Pizza and Games because you have an important question that you want to ask me?"

"Right," Max nodded, "now, you're getting it. I'm so glad you understand. Boy, it is nice to have that out of the way. I worried we'd never get to the point."

Pete glared. "You knocked me out of a tree."

"Only because I need your help." Max shrugged, adding, "should I tell you why I need your help? Or would you like to keep bringing up ancient history?"

"Ancient history?" Pete felt annoyed, and he let some of that agitation tinge his voice. "It was FIVE minutes ago."

Max shook his head. "It's like they say; time is relative and all that."

Pete glared. He would have said something, but he couldn't think of what to say. The only thing he could do was emote, and the emotion that swelled within him was anger.

"Oh, don't be like that." Max sighed. "I can send you back to your world. I can return you to before you climbed the tree to save me. You won't have to die." At this point, Max's voice went from lighthearted to menacing. "And believe me, you did die." Max let the words sink in—and for Pete, they did sink in—before reverting to his nonchalance. "But first, I need you to do something for me. Shall I tell you what that is?"

"You killed me?" Fear began to replace anger. Pete worried about his family; he felt disappointed that he would never know if Zoey liked him back. He thought she did, but it might have been his imagination. He had so much he wouldn't accomplish: graduate college, buy a house, have kids someday. Would he never do any of that? Wait, he told himself, realizing he was going about things the wrong way. "You said you can bring me back. In exchange, what do you need me to do for you?"

"I thought you'd never ask." Max's whiskers lifted to show pointed teeth beneath an arrogant smile. "That's very selfless of you." Pete didn't miss the sarcasm. "There is a world that needs you to save it."

"Save it from what?" Pete asked.

"My job is to send you there," Max explained. "Once there, you'll need to discover your purpose. At that point, you'll be able to grow in strength... become the hero that world needs."

"This is crazy." Pete shook his head. "You want me to go to a different world than my own, find my purpose, become a hero, and save that world? All this when I couldn't find my purpose in my own world?"

"Exactly," Max smiled. "I knew you were a bright one."

"And if I don't do it?" Pete raised an eyebrow.

Max squinted his eyes together, the smile on his face turning to a frown. "Then you stay dead, my boy. Your spirit moves on to whatever comes next. That could be better. It could be worse. Regardless, I have a world that needs a hero. Will you be that hero?"

The decision wasn't a difficult one to make. Pete wasn't ready to be dead. He'd do whatever he had to so he could return to his life. "Fine, I'll do it."

A smile returned to the cat's face, "good." And with that, the cat lifted his right arm, put his thumb and middle finger together, and snapped. A white light filled the room, blinding Pete and forcing him to close his eyes.

3: Greenlake

Blinding white...even with his eyes closed, he couldn't escape it. It filled every inch of his vision. Then, with the same suddenness with which it had filled the room, it was gone. And when he opened his eyes, he was no longer in a room.

Instead, he was cheek down, resting in a soft area of full, green grass. His mind was clear, his muscles energized. As he pushed himself up to a sitting position, he glanced left. The emerald grass extended a football field before it began to slope upward. From there, it became a series of waving hills and mounds. He noticed some cows and farm workers in that direction.

To his left, the hills became a tree-covered cliff face, rising hundreds of feet into the air. At the top of the cliff, a rock cropped out, forming a platform. He wondered if it was manmade or natural. Either way, it would provide a great view of the surroundings.

To the right, the hilly fields continued as far as he could see. A dirt road split the difference in terrain before turning to the right, running parallel in front of the hills. At the curve, a footpath branched out, winding up the forested incline.

He stood, looked in the other direction, and saw a body of reflective, dark water. Green islands and gray rocks poked out at irregular intervals, coming in all shapes and sizes. Straight ahead, his eyes couldn't see across the water. Though, the coastline wrapped around on the left and right. It made him think it was a large lake rather than an ocean. He could see a river to one side, a mountain range to the other. High up in the green mountain range, he thought he could see waterfalls. A snow-capped volcano highlighted the beauty of it all.

On the sloping terrain that ran down to the lake, at a distance of no more than fifty paces, someone had built a town. From his position in the outskirts of town, he could see the whole of it. Three streets ran parallel with the lake, spaced one block apart from each other. Many other streets ran up and down the slope, connecting the three longer streets. A single dirt road provided the only way in and out of town. It was the same road that he'd noticed near the wavey fields of green.

Other than for a large, yellow building, and a terminal with carriages, he couldn't tell the difference between a residence and a business. The design of everything reminded him of an old European town. It was something that might belong in a Disney movie or Grimm's Fairytales.

Pete would hesitate to call any of the structures a house. Instead, he felt inclined to call them cabins. He half expected a line of dwarves to leave one while carrying pickaxes over their shoulders.

No sooner had this thought entered his mind when he noticed a door open on one of the cabins. A line of bearded men exited the cabin. Where his distance from the town made it difficult to tell for sure, they seemed short and fat. He checked for pickaxes but didn't see any.

"Close enough," he whispered to himself, shrugging.

He watched other people in the town's streets. Where most of them were human, some were not. His eyes scanned around, identifying the races that he could: elves, dwarves, halflings, orcs, and gnomes. He could have sworn there were even pixies buzzing about, but he wouldn't be sure until he got closer.

"I have two questions for you, son," a gruff voice pulled him away from his thoughts, and he turned to its source. The man before Pete was human, clad from shoulder to toe in worn, steel armor. He held a shield in his left hand; a sword hung from his left hip. Well-groomed, brown hair sat atop his head, parted on the left. The bushy mustache over the man's lip reminded him of a caterpillar that seemed to crawl as the man spoke. "First, are you okay?"

Pete nodded.

"Good," the man sighed, "then, son, my second question is this… What in the name of the moderators are you wearing?"

Wearing? Pete's eyes widened in horror when he remembered his pantless, tank top look. He glanced down and sighed with relief. He was back in his pizza uniform.

"It's the uniform that my job gave me," Pete explained. When Pete said his first word to the guard, he noticed something strange. A name appeared above the guard's head. It read Nick Warman. Next to the name, Pete saw LVL 10. It reminded him of playing a massive multiplayer online role playing game but in real life. MMORPG's were his favorite games, so he thought it was cool.

"Job?" The guard repeated. Eyes squinting, he looked Pete's vestment up and down, an incredulous frown on his face. The eccentric mustache accented the expression. "And what kind of job do you do?"

"I work in food," Pete answered, pulling off his hat and pointing at the logo. "See. Pizza."

Josh Walker

"Pizza?" The guard shook his head. "I've never heard of that? Is it better than steak?" Before Pete could answer, the frown on the guard's face disappeared, and the guard began to laugh in a high pitched giggle. It was a weird contrast to his deep voice. "Of course, it isn't as good as steak. Nothing is as good as steak."

Did the man tell a joke and then laugh at his own joke? Pete couldn't tell for sure. "I'll have to make you a pizza sometime." Pete offered. "You might like it."

"It is possible," the guard began to regain his composure. "You stay out of trouble. Okay, son? I'm going to continue my rounds. Have a nice day. Welcome to Greenlake."

"Yeah," Pete said, "you, too." *Greenlake must be the name of the town*, he realized. *Seems appropriate.*

As the guard walked away, his armor clanked. Pete watched the clanking man for a few seconds. All the while, he wondered what to do next. The cat had said that Pete had to become a hero. How could he do that? As he contemplated these things, a fly landed on Pete's neck. By reflex, he swung his palm up, slapping...and connecting. At the same second he killed the insect, he heard a chime, and a text box appeared, filling his vision.

4: Flies Give One XP

Looking at the white words against the blue background, he read the prompt.

You defeated the fly! You gained one experience point!

While his eyes traced along with the words, an ominous voice spoke. He knew he was the only one who could hear it. Even so, it was loud and tangible, each word echoing. He reread the prompt, and the voice read with him.

You defeated the fly! You gained one experience point!

Then he decided to try something. He began at the beginning of the prompt again.

You defeated...

He stopped, and so did the voice. Then he read the prompt, again, repeating words and jumping back and forth between others. The voice read whichever word he did, creating a weird kind of beatbox.

You defeated... defeated... you...defeated... fly... defeated... You defeated the fly. Point. Point. Point. Defeated... defeated. You defeated the fly. Point.

Pete chuckled, amused with the makeshift song. Then he asked himself, "how do I close this window? He saw an X on a tab in the top right. Before he could figure out what to do with it, another prompt came, covering the first one.

You gained .5 slapping proficiency.

A third box appeared.

You gained .5 slapping defense.

Slapping defense? He wondered. *Did I raise my defense by slapping myself? If that's the case, building up my defense won't be difficult at all.* He slapped himself on the chest.

You gained .5 slapping proficiency. Slapping proficiency raises to level one.

You gained .5 slapping defense. Slapping defense raises to level one.

Pete continued to slap himself until his proficiency and defense both raised to level ten. At that point, he stopped receiving bonuses for slapping himself, so he stopped slapping himself; there is no point in slapping yourself if you don't get anything out of it.

Though he couldn't see straight ahead, not with all the prompts filling his vision. Out of the corner of his eye, he noticed some people staring at him. When Pete realized he had an audience, he tried to focus on something positive. At least he was wearing pants. That made his situation better than when he had been in the pizza and games with Max. So what if he was slapping himself?

Before he did anything else, he wanted to figure out how to close the prompts, so he tried a few things. First, he lifted his hand, trying to push at the tab with the X. It didn't work…he noticed more people watching him. "Gah," he whispered, no longer able to compartmentalize, grumbling about how much he hated when people watched him.

After poking his finger in the air didn't work, he tried using his whole hand. He tried pulling down from the tab. He tried staring at the X and willing the menu to close. Nothing worked.

Since he couldn't close the menus, he wondered if he could open his status screen. Once there, he figured he'd find a tutorial. The tutorial would show him how to close windows.

But how could he open his status menu? When he thought about it, a notification appeared.

Open status menu?

Yes, he said in his mind, hoping it would work to open the menu. A new prompt appeared over the last one:

Confirm opening status menu?

"Yes," he shouted aloud. "YES!" As he shouted, people continued to stare. He looked away from them, and after a short delay, his status menu opened.

His main status screen opened.

NAME: Pete   **RACE:** Human   **JOB:** Unknown

LEVEL 1

HP: 32/34

MP: 4/4

STR: 4
DEX: 7
VIT: 7
INT: 8
SPR: 5
AGI: 7

ALIGNMENT: Lawful Good
RELIGION: Christian
LANGUAGES: English,
Spanish,
Common
GENDER: Male
HEIGHT: 5'8
WEIGHT: 145 lbs
AGE: 20
EYES: Blue
Hair: Blond

LEFT ARM: Unequipped
RIGHT ARM: Unequipped
HEAD: Pizza Place Hat
BODY: Pizza Place Polo
LEGS: Black Jeans
FEET: No Slip Sneakers
HANDS: Unequipped
NECKLACE: Unequipped
EARRINGS: Unequipped
Ring 1:   Silver Claddagh
Ring 2:   Unequipped

ATTACK: 12
DEFENSE: 18
MAGIC ATTACK: 0
MAGIC DEFENSE: 6

PROFICIENCIES: Slapping Skill 10, Slapping Defense 10, Tree Climbing -5

Experience: 1/100

The part about the tree climbing seemed unnecessary to Pete. His low strength stat bothered him, too...and how did he lose two HP? He thought about it for a few seconds, realizing it must have happened when he slapped himself. If he kept slapping himself like that, could he slap himself to death? That would be an awful way to go.

He found the MP stat interesting. It signified he was in a world where magic existed. Where he wasn't sure what every attribute did, he had a good idea. Strength was his strength.

Dexterity would determine his fine motor skills. In some games, it influenced critical hit rates with all weapons or the accuracy of ranged weapons. He wouldn't be sure until he got a chance to test it.

Vitality would influence how well he could receive a hit, and it might have a direct impact on his hit points. In some games, it impacted how much stamina a person had. He searched for a stamina bar but didn't see one. Did this world not have stamina limitations, or was it not a measurable attribute? When he got a chance, he'd have to run and see if he got tired.

Intelligence was self-explanatory. It determined how smart he was. But he suspected it would also regulate his ability to cast spells. Would he be able to learn any spells? He convinced himself he would. After all, he was the hero of the world. He should be able to learn some magic. Where intelligence impacted a spell's power, spirit related to a person's spell resistance. That was its traditional purpose.

Agility would impact his speed and reflexes. His balance and stealth skill tied to the stat, too.

When he focused on each equipped item, its bonuses appeared in the blank space to the right of the attributes. Along with the bonuses, he saw a picture of the item.

His Pizza Place polo gave him a plus two defensive bonus. His ring gave him a plus three defense bonus and a plus-three to magic defense. He wondered if the silver in it provided more effective protection. His jeans gave him plus two to his defense. His shoes gave him a plus two. He wondered where his other defense points came from, guessing they tied to VIT and other factors.

His attack stat was more confusing for him to figure out. Each of his bare hands gave him a plus three damage bonus, totaling six. How that jumped to twelve was beyond him.

A scream sounded in the field, pulling his attention away from the menu.

5: When Nightshade Attacks

Pete tried to look in the direction of the scream, but the prompts blocked his vision. It was like staring into a blaring sun through smudged glass. He couldn't make out any detail.

Instead, he saw a shadow. So far as he could tell, the dark outline was human. It boasted a torso with two arms, two legs, and a small, round head. Each leg beat against the ground in a furious, panicked rhythm. Whoever it was, they were running.

He couldn't distinguish if they were running to something or away from something. If something was chasing them, it wasn't big enough to create a shadow that he could see through the prompts. What if it was invisible?

Did this world have invisible monsters? Pete wondered what other kinds of creatures he might encounter in the world. Were there Dragons?

The running figure screamed again, followed by pleas, "Help! It's gaining on me!" The voice possessed a definite feminine quality. Yet, the shrillness created by her panic made it difficult for Pete to determine an age.

Good thing the guard is nearby, Pete thought. Then he reconsidered. Was the guard nearby? Pete'd been slapping himself and examining his menus for a few minutes. Had the guard strayed too far away? What if no one else could help the woman? What if Pete was in danger? The thing could eat the woman, then it could come for him. Unable to see, he'd have no way to defend himself.

He tried to look left and right, hoping to see around the prompts...and it worked. Well, it kind of worked. He realized that when he glanced out of the side of his eye, He could see around the edges of the menu screens. It didn't give him a comprehensive view

of what happened, like looking through the crack between a door and its frame.

His eyes followed the woman as she fled. With
the wind blowing against her, her black pigtails and the
skirt of her dress trailed her. Pigtails shifted back and
forth like hungry snakes; her dress rippled like angry
waves.

Behind her, he could finally see her assailant. It
was short, no taller than her chest. Green vines formed
its body, thicker near its core, branching into a thin pair
of arms and legs. Dagger shaped leaves stuck out of
the vines, hiding much of its shape, including its head.

When Pete focused on the creature, he saw a
name appear above its head. Nightshade Terror LVL 1.
The letters were white with a black outline, making
them easy to read against the green mounds and sky-
line.

"Well, son," he heard the guard's voice ap-
proaching to his right. "This is no good."

"No, it's not." Pete agreed. Instead of turning to
the guard, he kept his narrow field of vision on the girl.
"Are you going to help her?"

"Grmmm…" Did the guard growl?

When there was no further response, Pete insisted, "you should go help her. Isn't that your job?"

"No," The guard sounded annoyed. The tone reminded Pete of a math teacher explaining a basic concept to a student, a concept that the student should already know. "It isn't my job. The city limit ends at the
field. My job is to guard the city. I am a city guard."

Pete thought about the words. He felt annoyed at
the guard's reluctance to help. "She needs someone to
save her, and you worry about jurisdiction?"

"Grmmm…" the guard grumbled again, waiting a
few seconds before adding. "I don't know what you
think my sub job is, son, but I'm not a gardener. In
fact, our town hasn't had a gardener since the night-

shade plants ate our last one. As it stands, no one has the qualifications to save her."

Qualified? Ate the last one? What kind of nonsense was that? "Are you saying," Pete asked, "that a level ten guard is afraid of fighting a level one plant?"

"Listen," The guard raised his voice. "I am a level ten guard, one of the few in the region. If I had permission, I could tear that monster to pieces with my bare hands and wear its remains as a necklace."

"So why don't you?" Pete egged on the guard, hoping it might provide the extra motivation to push him into action.

Instead, Pete received another, "grmmm." This one was louder and angrier than the previous grumbles. It was enough for Pete to turn his head and fix his limited field of vision on the guard. The guard's face was bright red; even his mustache looked angry. It made Pete feel uneasy, so he spun his vision back to the woman.

"Well," Pete inhaled a deep breath. "If you aren't going to do anything, I am."

"Wait," Pete heard the guard say as Pete began to run toward the woman.

It didn't take Pete long to realize he might have made a mistake. For one, the monster was the same level as him, and he didn't have a weapon with which to fight it. And without peripheral vision, he had to keep his head sideways as he ran, eyes to the side. Looking at everything that way was starting to give him a headache. Not to mention, running like that looked silly.

Even so, the woman needed help; he couldn't let her down. Instead of worry about the things that counted against him, he decided to recognize one thing that went in his favor. What was that thing? At least, it wasn't a raccoon monster. That fact gave him a fighting chance. If it were a raccoon monster, the woman would have been on her own. He hoped this new world didn't have raccoon monsters. He also hoped it didn't have raccoons.

His seven agility points helped him close the distance between himself and the monster and the girl. A flawless running technique also helped. He'd learned it from his high school track coach.

A prompt chimed. He let his eyes stray to it for a second, and it informed him he'd gained one point of proficiency in running. The ominous voice accompanied the prompt. His eyes went to the side again.

From his position, he was running at an angle to the woman. He tried to time it so he would breach the space between her and the monster. If he could accomplish that, he hoped he could draw the creature's attention away from her.

At twenty paces from the monster, he saw the monster's mouth for the first time. It was a gaping red maw with triangular teeth. It reminded him of an irate jack-o-lantern. Small black dots formed its beady eyes. "Over here," Pete shouted, not sure if he was yelling at the woman or at the nightshade plant. Either one would work.

Both ignored him.

With ten paces between them, he shouted again.

They continued to ignore him, but he could see the nightshade with greater detail. Hollow holes formed its ears. Leaves formed a collar around its neck. Hardened vine curled pointed fingers on each hand. With those hands, it reached for the woman, and it was gaining on her.

Pete willed himself forward, knowing he needed to reach them before it caught her.

At five long steps away, he made a last-second decision. He realized the space between the monster and the girl wasn't enough for him to get between them. Instead, he'd have to take on a new approach.

At one stride away, he lunged and slammed into the center of the monster: wrapping his arms around it, pulling it to the ground, and rolling to a stop. It was a tackle that would have earned him a spot as a varsity middle linebacker.

He received a new prompt chime but didn't take the time to read it. He guessed it related to tackling proficiency or something like that. Instead, he released the monster—he was confident he'd gained its attention—and rolled to his feet.

Then something remarkable happened; all his prompts closed. It allowed him to see straight ahead. Though, a new, transparent box appeared in the bottom left of his vision. It read:

You used tackle attack on Nightshade Terror. You caused 3 damage.

It is a battle log, he realized, recognizing it from the MMO's he'd played. A green health bar and purplish-pink mana bar appeared above the battle log. Transposed over the respective bars were the numbers 32/34 and 4/4.

As the monster stood, a slightly depleted red health bar appeared beneath its name. No numbers accompanied the bar. He could only guess at its HP.

Before he could process it all, the creature somersaulted toward him. As it closed the gap between them, it swiped.

The attack cut his exposed forearm, and the battle log read:

Nightshade Terror used slashing tendrils. You received 7 damage.

He flinched back, in part from reflex, in part from pain. The cuts burned, but they weren't too deep. At that moment, Pete's health bar went down; the corresponding number flashed from 32/34 to 25/34. When he saw this, his heart beat fast and heavy in his chest. His breathing accelerated. A bead of sweat formed on his brow. He didn't know what would happen if that twenty-five became a zero. At best, he'd fall unconscious. At worst, he'd die. If he died, something told him he wouldn't get to go back to earth.

"You'll pay for that," righteous indignation swelled within him as he glared at the monster in front of him. Then Pete did the only thing he could think to do. He'd played video games his whole life, and if there was one thing he learned from video games, it was to play to strengths. Pete only knew about one strength, so he decided to give it a try. He lifted his arm high over his head, palm open, and he slapped.

It wasn't a half slap like the ones he'd been doing on himself. He infused his attack with all the strength he could muster, and it connected with a loud whacking sound. It reminded him of the one time he had belly-flopped from the high dive.

After he'd carried out the attack, his eyes widened as he read the battle log:

You attacked. You caused 127 damage. You defeated the Nightshade Terror.

Across from him, the plant fell in a slump, forming a tangled mound of vines on the ground. At that moment, all the prompts from before returned: the status screen, the proficiency bonuses, the experience notification from the fly.

A few new prompts came to the forefront:

You defeated the Nightshade Terror! You gained 59 experience points.

You received two tomatoes.

You gained 2 slapping proficiency.

You gained .5 slashing defense.

Before he could read anything else, he heard the guard's voice behind him. "You've done it now, son." Did the guard sound angry? "I'm going to have to take you into custody." He did sound angry. "We can do this the hard way or the easy way."

Josh Walker

52

6: The No Leveling Clause

Pete chose the easy way, which meant he followed the guard to the mayor's office. Pete wasn't sure what the hard way might have been. Did it mean the guard would have tied a rope around his wrists and dragged him? Would the guard have lifted Pete like a sack of potatoes and carried him that way?

As Pete followed the guard through the streets of the town, he was able to get a close look at the buildings and houses. Almost every home had a picture frame window pointing in the direction of the lake. With the way the terrain sloped downward, Pete imagined each of those windows provided an excellent view.

The businesses—he realized—tended to be in short, wide buildings with a single story. They used batwing doors for the entrances with colorful signs by the doors. The signs indicated what business was inside: a bakery, a smith, an apothecary, a tailor, a jeweler, a carpenter, a general goods and supplies store, a specialty clothing boutique, a school, and an inn.

When they went by one store, he read its sign:

Wanda's Weird Windmill of Wonderous Widgets and Wild Waffler.

Through its windows, Pete noticed jars with glowing liquid, bright crystals, and shimmering bits of ore. Inside, a light shifted, casting strange rainbow-colored rays on the street outside. As impressive as it was, Pete wondered why they called it a windmill. It looked like a standard cabin to him.

Unlike the dirt road leaving town, most of the streets in town were gray brick. It amazed Pete how the masons who constructed the streets organized each of the bricks. They lined and packed the bricks where no edges poked up. With his foot, he couldn't feel where one brick ended and one began.

As Pete walked, he had to be careful because pedestrians filled the streets. When Pete saw those Pedestrians up close, he confirmed three things. First, most were human. Second, the group of bearded men that he saw leave the cabin were dwarf height. When he and the guard walked by them, they were whistling. Third, the bright lights that he'd seen before were pixies.

Green bushes, vines, and trees covered their whole town. And he also noticed red, funnel-shaped flowers growing from the vines and orange flowers sprouting from the bushes.

As beautiful as the town was, Pete felt disappointed. With all the prompts still blocking the center of his vision, having to aim his eyes to the side to see anything, he couldn't help but realize he was missing out.

The guard led Pete down two streets and over three. Then they came to a single-story cabin with fading white paint. Green shingles created the roof. They accented reddish-pink outlines around the windows. City planners designed the building so two rectangles met at their edges. It gave the edifice a distinct L shape. A single set of batwing doors rested in the longer rectangle. It provided the only visible way in and out of the building.

Near the doorway, flags blew. One of the flags was solid green with white lines forming a circle in the flag's center. The ringed border provided the frame for an image of a lake. He guessed the flag was Greenlake's.

A second flag had a royal blue background, golden thread forming dragons in each of the corners. The dragons appeared to be wingless and swimming with long narrow bodies. The center was the image of a castle's watchtower, sewn with the same gold.

The guard guided Pete past the flags and into the

doors. From there, they turned right, following the stem of the L to a closed door at the end of the hall. A plaque on the door read:

Mayor Yam Hopler

The guard knocked three, quick times. Knock, knock, knock. To accompany the knocks, he shouted, "It's Nick. This is urgent business."

"Come in." A woman's voice answered from the other side.

The guard pushed the door open, and Pete followed him in. It reminded Pete of the time he had to go to the principal's office when he was in Kindergarten. He didn't know it was against the rules to bring candy to class, but he learned his lesson. From then on, he always learned and worked to understand the rules. It was the first and last time he got in trouble at school.

Ordinary people make eye contact by looking straight ahead into the eyes of the person across from them. With the prompts, Pete couldn't do this. Instead, he stood with his left shoulder ahead of him, looking at the mayor out of the corner of his eye.

She sat at a wooden desk. It had four, square oak legs, connected by a center arch. A single heavy plank of what looked like the same wood formed a neat rectangular desktop. On it sat a book, some sheets of paper, and a quill dipped in ink for writing.

At first glance, he knew the woman wasn't human. She was shorter...rounder. A solid, red stocking cap rested atop her blond hair. A striped, blue shirt covered her stout body. Her round nose curled upward near the point. She was a gnome, he realized. Her wide, blue eyes stared back at him, blinking with confusion.

"I'm sorry," she glanced at the guard and spoke fast. It was like she was afraid she would run out of time to say what she wanted to say. "But what is he doing? Why is he looking at me like that? Is he broken? Did you break someone, again?"

The guard grumbled, but before he could do anything else, Pete answered. "I'm so sorry. I have a condition. I don't mean any offense by it." As soon as Pete spoke, the words Yam Hopler LVL 7 appeared above the woman's head. Pete decided he'd have to get used to people's names and levels being above their heads. It seemed like it would happen to everyone when he was talking to them.

"A condition?" Her eyes widened further. "Oh, gosh...is it contagious? Please, tell me it isn't contagious. I hope it's not contagious. Wait, who is he, anyway? Why did you bring him here? Is he a garbage man? Life in this town would be so much easier if we had someone with garbage man as their job. Wait...did the garbage make him contagious?"

"Unfortunately, he's not a garbage man. Also, he's not sick. From what I can tell, he's fine," the guard interrupted. "Aside from breaking one of the laws of the moderators."

Laws of the moderators? Pete wondered, what in the world is a law of the moderators?

"Oh, no," She frowned, wrinkles of concern coming to her face. Her eyes shifted back and forth between Pete and the guard. "Is he stuck with his eyes like that as a punishment? Which law did he break?"

Yeah, Pete wondered, turning his head to look at the guard, which law did I break?

"He performed an action outside the scope of his job duties." When the guard spoke, disappointment filled his words. His drooping mustache highlighted the sentiment.

Pete turned his attention back to the mayor.

The wrinkles in her forehead had deepened. Her

lower lip quivered. "And…" she hesitated, her fast words stuck in her throat, her eyes unblinking. "and…and…and… you are sure he's not looking at me like that to cause other trouble? Is he taunting me? No… Are you sure it isn't punishment?" Her eyes went back and forth before settling on Pete, "stop looking at me like that."

"I'm sorry," Pete took a step back, squaring his shoulders and inclining his head down. "I didn't mean to…never mind. I'll stare at the floor." Of course, he wasn't staring at the floor. He was staring at prompt about a .5 slashing defense proficiency.

"Do you know what you've done?" She asked. He sure didn't. "How could you be so reckless?"

"I'm sorry," Pete repeated. "I'm new here. I didn't know."

"Didn't know?" Her voice was softer, tinged with confusion. "You didn't know? How did you not know? Did you hit your head or something?"

"I did," Pete nodded, "when I fell out of a tree. There was a cat. It's a long story. Can you explain to me what I did? Can you explain why it's bad? Can you do it like you're explaining it to a child for the first time?"

"Are you serious?" She asked; he could feel her eyes go over to the guard, and she repeated the question to him. "Is he serious?"

"Based on my interactions with him and the strange clothes he's wearing," the guard sighed. "Yes, I believe he might have hit his head. It is the best explanation for why someone would act so reckless."

"Alright," she looked back to Pete, explaining. "The moderators want to maintain balance in the world. To do so, they don't want one person to become more powerful than any other person.

"The best way they can do this is by making one simple rule. You are only allowed to level up when it is a direct result of doing your job...or if by accident you do something like stepping on an ant. That is the only way you can gain experience."

"What happens when you break the rule?" Pete asked.

"When you break the rule?" The mayor considered the question. "It depends on how grievous the violation. In the past, the moderators have destroyed whole towns to punish one person."

"But if it relates to my job," Pete asked, "It's okay for me to do it?"

"Right," she answered, "so I need you to look me in the eye right now and tell me one thing. What is your job?"

"Well," Pete looked up, guessing where her eyes might be behind the prompt—he was looking about six inches to the left of her—and he answered. "I'm a pizzaman..." Along with his words, a prompt appeared:

Congratulations! You received a main job! Your job is pizzaman!

7: Job Pizzaman, Race Human

"Pizzaman?" The mayor rolled the word over in her mind. "That sounds made up." She turned to the guard. "I want you to use your analyze ability. Confirm if this is true."

"Sure thing," The guard agreed.

Pete could feel the guard's eyes on him, but more than that, he could feel something like static buzzing in his head.

He guessed it was the analysis spell. As the guard check Pete's job, Pete panicked. Even though he'd received the prompt saying he was a pizzaman, he hadn't seen if that carried over to his status page. Pete willed that status page to the forefront of his prompts, and he evaluated it.

NAME: Pete **RACE:** Human **JOB:** Pizzaman

LEVEL 1

HP: 25/34
MP: 4/4

ALIGNMENT: Lawful Good
RELIGION: Christian
LANGUAGES: English, Spanish, Common

STR: 4
DEX: 7
VIT: 7
INT: 8
SPR: 5
AGI: 7

GENDER: Male
HEIGHT: 5'8
WEIGHT: 145 lbs
AGE: 20
EYES: Blue
Hair: Blond

LEFT ARM: Unequipped
RIGHT ARM: Unequipped
HEAD: Pizza Place Hat
BODY: Pizza Place Polo
LEGS: Black Jeans
FEET: No Slip Sneakers
HANDS: Unequipped
NECKLACE: Unequipped
EARRINGS: Unequipped
Ring 1: Silver Claddagh
Ring 2: Unequipped

ATTACK: 12
DEFENSE: 18
MAGIC ATTACK: 0
MAGIC DEFENSE: 6

PROFICIENCIES: Slapping Skill 12, Slapping Defense 10, Tree Climbing -5, Running 1, Tackling 1, Slashing defense .5

Experience: 60/100

"He's not lying." The guard declared. "I see it on his status page, clear as undercooked egg whites. He is a pizzaman."

"Pizzaman?" The nervous mayor spoke even faster than before. "What's a pizzaman? I've never heard of a pizzaman. Nick, have you ever heard of a pizzaman?"

"I'm sad to say that I haven't." The guard answered. "Though, he did mention food to me before. He called it pizza. I didn't ask him about it because it isn't steak. When food isn't steak, eggs, or bacon, it isn't food."

"What's a pizzaman?" The mayor asked again.

With all the prompts in his way, Pete couldn't tell if she was asking him or the guard. When she repeated the question, he assumed the question was directed at him...

"A pizzaman makes pizza." He told her. "Sometimes a pizzaman brings pizza to people in their houses."

Within microseconds of finishing his answer, she began with another question. "And what's a pizza?"

"What is pizza?" Pete repeated the question, confused. Who doesn't know what pizza is? "I don't understand. You've never had pizza?"

"She gets to ask the questions, son," the guard told him. "You get to answer. Tell her now. What is pizza?"

"Right," Pete took a few seconds to consider before he answered. "You take a ball of something like bread dough and flatten it into a disc. That disc is the crust. Sometimes people season the crust with garlic, butter, salt, and other spices. Sometimes the crust is thick like bread. On occasion, it is thin and crispy like a cracker.

"Once you have a crust, you crush tomatoes into a sauce. If you want, you can add things to the sauce to flavor it. Once you've made the sauce, you spread it over the crust." Pete was starting to feel hungry. "From there, you sprinkle grated cheese over the sauce. You can add other things to the pizza, too, like little slices of meat or peppers. Some people put the toppings on top of the cheese. Others like to put toppings under the cheese."

"Steak sounds better." The guard declared. "But I like the part about slices of meat. Can you add sausage? Bacon?"

"You can make a meat pizza with all the meats," Pete confirmed.

Though Pete didn't see it, the guard nodded his approval. "That makes me happy. Good work, son."

"Tomato?" The mayor's expression began to relax. "You need tomatoes to make pizza? Is that why you killed the nightshade plant? You needed to get tomatoes?"

"What?" Pete asked, not understanding, trying to process. Then he remembered the two tomatoes the nightshade plant had dropped. Then he remembered that tomato plants are a type of nightshade. It all came together for Pete, and he understood.

"That makes sense," the guard said. "You saw the girl in trouble, and you wanted to help her. When you realized you needed the tomatoes for your pizza, you knew you could help her because getting tomatoes was part of your job." The guard dropped his hand on Pete's shoulder. "I'm sorry I doubted you."

"Uh," Pete mumbled. "No problem…"

"No hard feelings, right." Pete turned back, so his limited field of vision was on the guard. Now, the mustache appeared happy, turned up at the corners like it was a smile or something. "That was brave of you to save her. Good work, son. But why did you act like you have amnesia? You could have said you were doing your job."

"About that…" Pete began.

"Can you kill the other tomato plants, too?" The mayor interrupted. "Of course, they'll respawn again. Even so, it takes them a few days to reach the town from their respawn point. Since you need tomatoes, you can keep hunting them, right? Keep them away from the town?"

Another prompt filled Pete's vision:

You have been offered the quest, "Nightshade Slaughter." Completion reward: 100 len, 200 experience points. Do you accept the quest?

As he read the prompt, the ominous voice accompanied it. He wondered what determined if the voice would accompany a prompt because it didn't come for all of them. From what he could tell, it appeared for non-combat pop-up prompts. He'd have to test it out later.

Pete reread the prompt, ominous voice accompanying the reading… And Pete considered the quest rewards. He didn't know what len was, but he guessed it was some type of currency. He didn't know if 100 of it was a lot or not. More impressive was the 200 experience points.

Between that and the individual experience from each monster, he could gain at least two levels from the quest. He wondered how leveling up would work but didn't spend too much time thinking about it.

"Two things," Pete began. "First, I did fall out of a tree, hit my head, and I can't remember everything, so please be patient when I have questions."

"Okay," the mayor answered, asking. "What is the second thing."

"Second," Pete adjusted his hat before scratching his cheek and continuing. "I accept. I'll kill the Nightshade plant."

The prompt changed:

You have accepted the quest, "Nightshade Slaughter." Put an end to the malignant plants and begin your journey as a pizzaman.

8: The Nightshade Slaughter

"**B**efore I go kill the nightshade creatures, I need to ask one of those questions about something I forgot," Pete told the mayor.

"Oh," The mayor interlocked the fingers of her hands, resting them on her desk. She used her arms to support herself as she leaned forward. The tone of her voice reminded Pete of a psychiatrist about to help a patient. He wasn't sure if it was sincere compassion in her voice. Rather, it seemed more like concern...like she understood there was a problem, a problem she would be responsible for solving. "What question is that?"

"This is embarrassing," he inhaled, hoping they wouldn't be harsh in their judgment of him. "I've forgotten how to close my prompt windows."

The mayor stared at him, unmoving aside from for her eyes that widened each time she blinked. "You forgot...how to close...your prompts?"

"That is embarrassing." The guard let out a deep belly laugh, arms over his stomach. "I'm not sure what is worse, forgetting how to close the prompt window or being stuck in those silly clothes."

"You're serious?" The mayor asked. She blinked a few more times before she continued. "You forgot how to close your prompt windows?"

Pete nodded, "it's why I keep looking at you out of the side of my vision. I can't remember how to close the prompts."

"You're not serious," she let out a nervous laugh before forcing sternness into her voice. "Or are you?" Pete hung his head. "Moderators, you are serious."

The guard continued to howl with laughter.

Pete hung his head. "I'm sorry. When the cat knocked me out of the tree, I fell. I don't remember anything. I don't even know the name of the land I'm in. Moderators," Pete decided to adopt the word he'd heard both the mayor and the guard use before he continued. "I don't even know the name of this world."

He hoped using the terminology, 'this world,' wouldn't confuse the others. *Moderators*, he realized, *there are more worlds than this one and Earth. There is no way these are the only two.* If that was the case, how many worlds were there?

"Well, this is a lot to take in," The mayor told him. "Please, don't feel judged. We can help. Let me answer all your questions."

"He should feel judged," The guard was turning red with laughter.

The mayor shot the guard a glare before refocusing on Pete and continuing. "The name of our country is Lakes. The world you are in is Round." Pete began to realize how literal the names were in Round. "As far as closing the window goes, you look at the tab with the X, will the prompt closed, and close your eyes with force."

The second she explained the processes, Pete closed the prompts, blinking his eyes over and over. The first prompt he closed was the one about slashing resistance; the last one he closed was about the fly giving him one experience point.

With his vision cleared, he looked back at the mayor. "Thank you so much. That was starting to give me a headache. Now, tell me. Where can I find these nightshade plants?"

The guard guided Pete to the same part of town where they'd met before. From there, they took the footpath that wound behind the cliff face and ascended. Along the path, at the hill's base, there were a few trees with narrow trunks. Yet, the higher up the mountain they went, the more trees there were, and the trees became taller, wider at the base. After only a few minutes, Pete felt like he was on a forest path. It reminded him of camping in the Rocky Mountains as a kid.

"The plants spawn at the top of this hill, near the

outcropping along the cliff." The guard explained. "For their own protection, they like to stay in a group. When you find one of them, you're likely to find them all."

"I see…Nick…that's your name, right? Can I call you Nick?"

"It is my name." The guard named Nick nodded.

"Okay, then, Nick." Pete began, asking. "What about the plant that attacked the woman? Why wasn't it with the group?"

"Sometimes, they get separated." He shrugged. "Either way, they always find their way to town."

"And you have to wait for them to go into town before you can kill them?" Pete asked.

"That's where I'm allowed to kill them." Nick nodded. "Good thing a pizzaman is here. If not, the creatures might have doomed the town to withstand their perpetual attacks until the end of time."

"Good thing," Pete agreed. He'd never received such praise while working as a pizzaman on Earth. He was beginning to like the town of Greenlake in the country called Lake in a world named Round. "I had one other question."

"Grmmm…" Nick grumbled. "You talk a lot."

Pete ignored the comment, asking, "Why did you arrest me? You can only do guard stuff inside the city. You threatened to detain me outside the city. Was that a bluff?"

Nick turned to Pete, "moderators, you don't remember anything, do you?" Pete shook his head, so Nick continued speaking, both men walking side-by-side up the narrowing, muddy pathway. "When someone breaks one of the rules of the moderators, it is a person's civic duty to detain them. The moderators would have granted anyone the authority to arrest you at that moment."

"I see," Pete understood, pushing his shoulder blades back to stretch as he walked. "You happened to be the one that saw me kill the plant, so you were the one that detained me."

"The girl you saved saw you, too," Nick said. "If I didn't detain you first, she would have."

"Seems ungrateful of her." Pete finished stretching his shoulders.

Nick rolled his eyes. "No one upsets the moderators. They rule this world." Nick stopped, extending his arm in front of Pete, forcing Pete to stop next to him. "Wait, I see them." Using the same arm he'd used to stop Pete, Nick pointed to a clearing ahead of them and to the right.

Sure enough, five of the creatures roamed the area. They didn't walk like regular animals. In a way, they reminded Pete of a doll or puppet in a television show, bopping up and down with each step. All the while, an offscreen puppeteer moved them from one position to another. Only, these were real. There were no strings.

Their arms hung at their sides as lifeless vines. When he noticed their hands, he saw each creature had a different number of clawed fingers. Some had three fingers to a hand, one had at least twenty. Their leaves remained flat against their bodies. It allowed Pete to see their round, red heads with clarity.

The names above their head and level indicators showed that four of the five were level one. The one with lots of fingers was level two.

He didn't know how he didn't realize it before, "their heads are tomatoes." Pete whispered, resisting the urge to hum the theme song for Attack of the Killer Tomatoes. It was an old cartoon he used to watch. The cartoon based itself on an even older movie.

"Do you think you can kill all five?" Nick asked. "In the mayor's office—when I checked your status—your hit points weren't at full."

"Do you have something that can get my hit points back up?" Pete asked. "A potion or something?"

Nick muffled a laugh, no doubt to keep the nightshade monsters from hearing him. "A potion. That's funny. What makes you think I can afford something like a potion? You'll have to sleep back your HP like the rest of us."

"What do you mean the rest of us?" Pete asked. "Is the only way people get their hit points back by sleeping? Or are there potions?"

"There are potions," Nick continued to stave off laughter. "They cost 500 len a piece. No one in Greenlake can afford to spend that much on a single item. Though, I hear Wanda's sells them."

Pete considered Nick's words, wondering if he should rest before taking on the plant monsters. Before he made the decision, he needed to ask Nick one more question. "Do you know if the nightshade terrors link when you attack one?"

"Link?" Nick lifted an eyebrow. "What does link mean?"

"If I attack one," Pete clarified, "will the others attack me in response?"

"Only if they see you," Nick told him.

"Good to know." Pete made his decision. "I am confident I can fight them now. Wait here."

"One way or another, this should be entertaining." Nick smiled at Pete as Pete snuck off the path, moving through the bushes, inching toward the clearing where the plants wandered.

All the while, he observed the plants, wondering if there was a pattern to their movements. He hoped he'd see something he could exploit. If he could predict their actions, he could ambush them one at a time without drawing the others' attention.

Unfortunately for Pete, there was no repetition, no model which allowed him to guess where one might move. The actions of the plants were beyond erratic. He wasn't even sure what motive they had for their meandering.

Pete came to the clearing's edge, a thin layer of foliage between him and the creatures, and he waited, watching as the big one stomped by his hiding spot. The one Pete had fought before was shorter than a person, but the big one appeared taller than a human. He could hear its spindly feet crunching over the forest's detritus, composed of dry, dead leaves with some small, broken branches.

Pete had killed the previous plant with one slap, but he wasn't confident he could do the same to the large one. So he let it go past him, waiting for one of the smaller ones to draw near. Before that happened, minutes passed, and they felt like hours.

He could feel the adrenaline spurting through his body. His muscles tightened; his hands were shaky; he could feel his energized heart thumping with a resilient vigor and steady rhythm. Pump. Pump. Pump.

Then, a small one neared his direction, and the others were on the opposite side of the clearing. He felt confident they wouldn't see what he was about to do. "Here goes nothing," he whispered, hopping out from his hiding spot. He landed straight-legged, shoulders square, facing the plant, and it froze in place.

He used its hesitation to his advantage, raising his hand high over his head and swinging it down, whacking across the plant's crown.

It dropped in a slump as prompts appeared:

You attacked. You caused 131 damage.

You defeated Nightshade Terror! You gained 39 experience points!

You received one tomato.

You gained .2 slapping proficiency.

Pete smiled. By his math, he was one experience point away from leveling up, but he knew he couldn't celebrate yet. With two quick—albeit forceful—blinks, he closed the prompts, returning to his hiding place behind the bush.

When another small one neared, he jumped in

front of it, his hand raised and ready to strike…

…It didn't freeze in place like the other. Instead, it attacked him, flashing its clawed hand in his direction, tearing through the fabric of his shirt and cutting across his stomach.

In an instant, he felt a sensation unlike any he'd ever felt before. It was a combination of numbness, pressure, and pain all at once. He winced, and a prompt appeared:

Nightshade Terror used slashing tendrils. Critical hit. Received 17 damage.

"Crap," Pete grunted, doing the math in his head. He was down to 8 hit points. One or two more hits would be the end of him. He'd have to kill the plant in front of him, flee, and come back for the other plants later.

His eyes fell upon his opponent, and he chambered his hand. But before he could slap, the creature opened its jack-o-lantern mouth and shrieked. It was an awful, high-pitched ringing sound like a tornado siren. The other three plants turned toward him and sped in his direction. Their arms reached out like zombies in search of brains. Within five seconds, they'd cross the clearing and be on him. He knew he needed to get out of there.

Pete swung his hand across the plant. Before it dropped…before he knew if he'd killed it or not…before any prompts appeared…he turned and began to run. His abdomen hurt, but he tried to ignore the pain.

It reminded him of playing lava monster at recess. He was the only one left alive; all his friends were after him. Of course, in lava monster, they wouldn't hurt him if they caught him. The only consequence was that he'd be the lava monster at the start of the next game. These plants chasing him was much worse. If they caught him, it would mean his end.

Two elongated strides into his escape, Pete saw

a new prompt appear:

You attacked. You caused 98 damage.

He took another stride, and a second prompt came:

You defeated Nightshade Terror! You gained 40 experience points!

He continued to run as other prompts came:

Congratulations! You gained a level!

As this prompt appeared, a chime sounded, and the pain Pete felt in his stomach disappeared. The instantaneous nature of it confused him. How did he go from feeling so much pain to feeling fine? It was like being sick with a temperature and the worst case of the flu one second and fine the next. It went against the laws of biology. What happened?

Did leveling up restore my hit points? Pete wondered. In many of the games he had played, HP would return to full every time a character gained a level. He needed to check his status sheet to make sure.

While still running, he pulled up the status screen and looked at his HP… … …it was full, and it maxed at a higher number than before. A sigh of relief escaped his lips. He wanted to look at his other attributes, but he knew that would have to wait. He blinked the status screen away, and a final series of prompts appeared:

You received three tomatoes.

You gained 3 slashing defense.

You gained 3 light armor proficiency.

You gained .3 slapping proficiency.

He blinked away the prompts as he slowed to a stop and turned to face the monsters that chased him. The level 2 plant had separated itself from the others, and he stood in place, still and waiting.

As it brought its arm back to swing at him, Pete dove to the side, rolling to his feet:

Nightshade Terror used slashing tendrils. Missed.

Pete lunged, swinging his hand across the monster:

You attacked. You caused 70 damage.

You defeated Nightshade Terror! You gained 77 experience points.

You received three tomatoes.

You gained .5 slapping proficiency.

You gained 2 running proficiency.

Pete made quick work of the remaining two tomato plant monsters. With the threat neutralized, he took the time to look at his status sheet.

NAME: Pete   **RACE:** Human   **JOB:** Pizzaman

LEVEL 2

HP: 45/50

MP: 5/5

STR: 8
DEX: 7
VIT: 10
INT: 10
SPR: 6
AGI: 9

ALIGNMENT: Lawful Good
RELIGION: Christian
LANGUAGES: English, Spanish, Common
GENDER: Male
HEIGHT: 5'8
WEIGHT: 145 lbs
AGE: 20
EYES: Blue
Hair: Blond

LEFT ARM: Unequipped
RIGHT ARM: Unequipped
HEAD: Pizza Place Hat
BODY: Pizza Place Polo
LEGS: Black Jeans
FEET: No Slip Sneakers
HANDS: Unequipped
NECKLACE: Unequipped
EARRINGS: Unequipped
Ring 1: Silver Claddagh
Ring 2: Unequipped

ATTACK: 36
DEFENSE: 33
MAGIC ATTACK: 0
MAGIC DEFENSE: 9

PROFICIENCIES: Slapping Skill 13.2, Slapping Defense 10, Tree Climbing -5, Running 3, Tackling 1, Slashing defense 4, Light Armor 4.2

Experience: 109/200

9: Leveling up

Pete guessed the attribute bonuses were more generous when they related to his proficiency gains. To be specific, his slapping proficiency and tackling were both skills related to strength. It seemed the four increase to his strength had a subsequent relationship to those skills.

In much the same manner, his light armor, slashing defense, and slapping defense related to vitality. Vitality went up by three points, more than the other attributes aside from strength.

His agility increased by two; he guessed this was due to the increase in running proficiency.

Since no one had used magic against him, his spirit gained one point. It seemed insignificant, but any increase was to his benefit.

What he couldn't figure out was why his intelligence jumped by two. He hadn't used any magic, nor had he performed any feats of cognitive greatness. He had learned no new spells, gained no intelligence-based proficiencies.

Where he couldn't be sure about anything, he made mental notes about the increases and closed the status screen. Then he looked around for Nick the guard. "Nick, are you out there? That was the last of them."

A finger tapped his shoulder from behind, and he jumped forward, spinning in the air, lifting his hand and preparing to slap.

It was Nick, standing there with his head cocked in confusion. "Are you okay, son? You seem a bit high strung."

"Sorry," Pete answered, lowering his hand and taking a deep, calming breath. "I didn't realize you were there."

"You should be careful where you open up your

status, inventory, and job skills screens," Nick advised. Pete wondered about the job skills and inventory screens. "If you get too involved looking at your advancements, anyone can sneak up on you. The next time it happens, the person—or thing—that sneaks up on you might not be as handsome and charming as me. Also, that person or thing might want to kill you. It could leave you in a bad place. Son, it could leave you in a dead place. And from that, there is no coming back."

"Right," Pete listened to the advice and decided it made sense. In the future, he'd make sure no one was around before he went through his screens. He hoped he'd have a chance to look at the job skills screen and inventory screens soon but knew it wasn't the time. "Let's get back to the mayor's office and let her know we took care of the nightshade plants."

Back in the mayor's office, the mayor remained sitting at her desk. Across from her, Pete stood side by side with Nick the guard, Nick explaining. "You should have seen it. At first, he slapped one. Then one scratched him. Then he slapped it and ran like a scared child. Then he stopped running and slapped the others. It was great entertainment."

"I'm confused," the mayor blinked. "Does that mean he defeated them? Moderators, why did he slap them? Why didn't he use a sword?"

"Sword?" Pete lifted his eyebrow. "I could have had a sword?" He turned to Nick. "Why didn't I get a sword, Nick?"

Nick muffled a chuckle before answering with a shrug. "You never asked for one."

"Never asked for one?" Pete glared. He could feel his anger building. Then he stilled his temper, realizing that it could be for the best. Even with a sword, he had no sword proficiency. His slapping attacks might be more potent than his sword attacks. Did Nick the guard realize this?

If that was the case, Nick did Pete a favor by not giving Pete a sword. Though Pete didn't appreciate Nick's laughter, he realized it wasn't the time or place to get back at Nick. Pete would wait for the perfect time and get his revenge in a more appropriate manner. A smile crept across Pete's face.

"Why is he smiling like that?" The mayor asked with her characteristic fast talk. "It's creepy. I don't like it. Make him stop."

Pete hurried to wipe the smile from his face, adopting a more neutral expression, and looking back at the mayor. "Sorry, I thought of something funny." Nick tilted his head to the right, suspicious of Pete, but he didn't say anything as Pete continued to talk. "As Nick explained, I did defeat the nightshade monsters. I slapped because I have experience with slapping. You see, a pizzaman has to slap the dough into a disc. It gives us lots of practice with slapping. It made it where a sword might not be the best option for fighting monsters."

"That makes sense." The mayor agreed, nodding. "Regardless, the town of Greenlake owes you a great debt. We are glad to have someone who can hold the nightshade monsters at bay. As they respawn, will you continue to accept responsibility for them?"

Pete nodded. "I will."

"Good," she smiled. "Then we thank you for your service. Please, accept your reward."

A prompt chimed:

You have completed the quest Nightshade Slaughter. You have begun your journey toward Pizzamandom.

Pizzamandom? Pete didn't think that was a real word. Two more prompts appeared:

You received 200 experience points.
Congratulations! You gained a level!

You earned 100 len.

After Nightshade Terrors respawn, return to the mayor's office to repeat the quest.

You completed a job-related quest. You receive 3 bonus job points.

This reminded Pete that he still needed to look at his job skill page and inventory page.

You have unlocked the quest Gathering Ingredients. It is the second quest in the pizzaman series. Completion reward: 200 len, 250 experience. Do you accept the quest?

Pete wondered about the new quest. It didn't give any specific details about what it entailed. Though, the name seemed self-explanatory. Aside from tomatoes, what else would he need before he could make some pizzas? Only one way to find out. He used his mind to answer yes to the question, accepting the quest:

You accepted the quest Gathering Ingredients. Unify the following ingredients and create the first pizza in Round: tomatoes x3, cheese x1, pizza dough x1, pizza fork x1, pizza peel x1, pizza cutter x1.

You have acquired 3 tomatoes. 1/6 ingredients needed for quest Gathering Ingredients. Gather the remaining five ingredients to complete the quest.

Pete blinked through the prompts before turning his attention back to the mayor. She sat at her desk, eyes blinking, an inquisitive expression on her face. "I'm sorry. Did you need something else? If you want, you can leave now. I mean. Don't think I'm kicking you out. Did you need something else?"

"In reality," Pete smiled, "I do have one question. Where can I get some cheese?"

10: Gathering Ingredients

Nick the guard guided Pete the Pizzaman to the Greenlake general goods store. They stopped outside, and Nick said. "I hope you find all the ingredients you need, son. Don't forget that you owe me a pizza with all the meats on it."

"As soon as I can track down the ingredients to make one, you'll be the first to try it." Pete agreed.

"Very good," Nick smiled, patting Pete on the shoulder. "Have a nice day. Stay out of trouble."

"Right," Pete told him. "I promise to stay out of trouble. Thanks for your help."

The guard nodded, rotated on his heel, and marched away.

Before Pete went into the general goods store, he decided he should check his inventory page. Before he did, he glanced left and right to make sure the street was clear. Then he willed it to open, and it responded, and he looked at it. His inventory included 13 tomatoes, a red gel pen, a black gel pen, a receipt from the last time he filled up his car with gas, a cell phone, 74 dollars, 28 cents, and 100 len.

Then he opened his job skills page. In the top left corner, the page read Pizzaman Job - Novice Skill Tree. In the top right, he saw he had 12 job points to allocate. The tree consisted of a single triangle in the center of the page. The word Pizzaman was in the triangle. From the triangle, three lines sprouted at the points, one going straight up, and two angled down and to the sides.

When he focused on the triangle, a prompt appeared:

Unlock Pizzaman Novice Skill Tree. Cost to unlock: 4 job points. Do you wish to Unlock Pizzaman Novice Skill Tree?

"Yes," he told the prompt with his mind.

Skill tree unlocked.

A circle appeared, connected to the triangle by the line pointing up. The word Fire appeared inside the circle. When he focused on the word, a description appeared:

Summon a small cooking flame. Spell Cost 1 MP. Cost to unlock: 3 job points. Do you wish to unlock Fire?

"No," he told the prompt. He wanted to look at his other options before he made any other choices.

A pentagon connected to the line going down and to the right. Heat Resist appeared inside the pentagon. He focused on the words and read the corresponding prompt:

Grants a permanent 20% heat resistance to survive hours by the oven. Cost to unlock: 3 job points. Do you wish to unlock Heat Resist?

That was amazing. He'd spent many summer nights by a hot oven. Plus, being 20% resistant to heat would come in handy if he ever faced a fire breathing dragon. Not to mention, it was a permanent resistance. He didn't have to cast it or use it as some unique ability. Even so, he still had one more option to evaluate before he made any choices. "No," he closed the prompt.

The line going down and to the left connected to a square with the words, 'Steel Hands,' inside it. He opened its corresponding prompt:

Use ability Steel Hands to double your slapping proficiency for thirty seconds. Slap perfect pizza dough every time. Cooldown sixty seconds. Cost to unlock three job points. Do you wish to unlock Steel Hands?

Pete paused to consider. The cost to unlock all three abilities was nine job points, but he only had eight left. He'd have to pick two of them. Lucky for him, it wasn't a tough decision. He reopened Fire, selecting to unlock it. When he did, a line extended up from the Fire ability, connecting to a new circle. Milk to Cheese appeared inside the new circle. The ability allowed him to turn a quart of milk into a block of cheese for one MP. It would cost his remaining five job points to unlock it. He considered it, but only for a moment. He closed the milk to cheese prompt.

Then he opened Heat Resist, allocating three points into the skill. As had happened before, a new line extended from the skill. At the end of the line, a pentagon appeared. The Pentagon offered the ability Cut Resist.

In his years at Pizza Place, he'd cut his hands on the pizza cutters and some prep knives, so he understood where the skill could be useful.

Though, Cut Resist was not as impressive as the other skill that had appeared. When he learned Heat Resist, simultaneously forming lines extended from Fire and Heat Resist, meeting to form a circle. The Circle read, 'Strong Fire.' It was a more robust version of the spell he'd already learned. It also cost more MP to use.

He sighed, knowing he wouldn't make any more job point purchases and closed the job skill menu. Then he looked up at the General Store in front of him.

Varnished logs formed its natural exterior walls. Its entrance came in the form of a tall, green door made from tin. The green matched the shingles of its roof. Pete pushed on the door and stepped inside.

Three rows of shelves ran the length of the

store, dividing it into four aisles. Where the shelves held food and drinks, rope and other supplies hung along the walls. A checkout clerk—a dwarf with a dark beard and big brown eyes—sat behind the counter to the right. Pete tipped his hat to the clerk as he entered in.

"Let me guess." The clerk smiled at him. "you need some string to fix your shirt?"

Pete glanced down at the hole in his shirt that the tomato plant monster had caused. He'd almost forgot about the hole. Even so, the tear didn't bother him. He'd need to upgrade to something that protected him better than simple cloth, and the sooner he did, the better.

"Actually," Pete told the clerk. "I need whatever you have of the following: a pizza cutter, a pizza fork, a pizza peel, cheese, and pizza dough."

"I have cheese." Clerk wrinkled his nose and pointed his lips to the side. "I don't know what those other things are."

"I'll take the cheese then," Pete answered. "Where in town would I find cooking tools?"

The Dwarf thought before responding. "Joey will have those."

"Who's Joey?" Pete asked.

"He's the smith."

"What about a wooden dowel? One about four feet long?" Pete was beginning to realize the general store was far from the supercenter chain stores he'd experienced back home.

"Carpenter'll have those." The Clerk shrugged. "Do you want me to grab you the cheese, though?"

"Yes," Pete nodded. "Thank you so much. How much is that by the way?"

"Five len a block." The clerk told him.

"Could you please get me five?" At that moment, Pete came to a horrifying realization. He didn't know how to get to his money. Sure, he had the United States money in his pocket, but the len transferred direct to his inventory. He wasn't sure how to access it. How could he buy something when he couldn't reach his money? Something told him the Dwarf would not accept Earth money.

"Five blocks of cheese," The Dwarf repeated. "Sure thing."

The clerk returned to his spot behind the counter, placing a bag with cheese on the counter, and a prompt appeared:

Transfer five blocks of cheese to inventory for 25 len?

Pete sighed, realizing he'd been worrying for nothing. Spending money in Round was even easier than spending it on Earth. On Round, he didn't even have to dig for his wallet.

When Pete selected yes, the cheese blinked out of existence from atop the counter, and Pete checked his inventory. Sure enough, it had five blocks of cheese and twenty-five less len. As he closed his inventory, a prompt appeared:

You have acquired 5 blocks of cheese. 2/6 ingredients needed for quest Gathering Ingredients. Gather the remaining ingredients to complete the quest.

Pete bid farewell to the clerk and made his way through town until he came to the smith. Unlike the general goods store, the smith's workstation was outside. The station was a fire next to an anvil. The smith sat there and used a pair of tongs in his left hand to hold a narrow piece of glowing red metal against the anvil.

With his right hand, he beat a hammer against the metal to shape it. Then he'd lift the metal with the tongs and dip it in cold water. When the hot metal touched the water, the water hissed like a snake, sending steam into the air. After a few cycles of this, the smith spoke, "Are you going to stand there all day and watch me?" He had a Scottish accent. "Or are you going to tell me what you need?"

"Sorry about that," Pete told him, stepping forward. "I didn't mean to lurk, but I didn't want to interrupt your work."

"I can work and talk." The Smith answered. "What do you need?"

"It's something specific. I'm not sure you've made something like it before. Do you know what a peel is? Or a pizza fork?"

"I'm not familiar with a pizza fork," He continued to hammer. "Tell me more about it."

"The pizza fork has a head that is a two-pronged fork, curved at a slight angle in one direction. Each prong is about the same length as a finger." Pete curved his pointer and middle finger to imitate the shape. "You take that head and put it on a long dowel."

"Sounds simple enough." The smith used the tongs to dip his current project in water, creating more steam. "You need me to make the metal forkhead part?"

"I do." Pete nodded. "And I need the peel, too."

"Is it a simple bread peel?" The smith put down his tools and the metal on which he worked, and he stretched. "A wide piece of metal with a handle that bakers use to pull bread out from the oven?"

"That's it." Pete nodded, holding up his hands about sixteen inches apart. He would have said sixteen inches, but he wasn't sure what units of measurement people used in Round. "I need one with an arm length handle and a head that is about this wide and long."

"I can make those things." The smith said.

"I'll need one more thing, too." Pete knew he'd

have a difficult time explaining what a pizza cutter looked like and how it functioned. He had a way to work around that, though. "But I need to show you a picture of it."

"A picture?" The dwarf smiled. "I do love pictures. My mom was a painter."

"It isn't quite a painting," Pete explained, removing his phone from his pocket and checking its battery. It still had a 70% charge. "This is a magic box. I need to show you…"

"That isn't magic." The smith cut him off. "That is a communication box. I have one myself." The dwarf reached into his pocket, removing a smartphone.

"Oh," Pete hesitated, surprised at the development. "Everyone in Greenlake has communication boxes?"

The smith laughed, "you are a strange one. Show me your picture."

Pete opened his photos and showed the smith an image of the pizza cutter, explaining how it worked.

"I can make that, too." The smith explained. "For everything you need, it'll cost 50 len. On the peel and cutter, I'll wrap their handles with a rubber grip, so you don't get burned while using them." The smith cast Pete a questioning glance. A glance that asked, you do have enough to pay, right?

Pete did have enough to pay but paying 50 len would bring his total money down to 25. Would 25 len be enough to buy dough from the baker and a shaft for the fork from the carpenter? He'd have to worry about that bridge when he got to it. "I have enough to pay," Pete confirmed.

"Good," The smith smiled. "I'll have your commission done in 30 minutes. You can wait in the corner or come back after it's done."

Pete chose to wait in the corner.

The smith only needed twenty minutes to finish. When he handed Pete the items and Pete chose to buy them, new prompts appeared:

You have acquired a pizza peel 3/6 ingredients needed for quest Gathering Ingredients. Gather the remaining ingredients to complete the quest.

You have acquired a pizza cutter. 4/6 ingredients needed for quest Gathering Ingredients. Gather the remaining ingredients to complete the quest.

Ten minutes after that, Pete arrived at the carpenter. The carpenter's shop was much like the general store. Though, it was a more expansive building with a tin door, shelves forming aisles, filled with things to buy.

Unlike the general store, the carpenter's shop had no one at its counter. While Pete searched for someone to help him, he examined some of the things in the store.

There were wooden snakes and other animals that swayed with realistic movements. They had a thin piece of wood down their center, rounded pieces of wood glued to it on each side. He saw small carvings of animals and flowers. All of it looked so real.

"Can I help you?" A woman's voice pulled him away from his browsing.

He looked at the woman, and her beauty caused his IQ to drop twenty points. He never was good at talking to someone who he found pretty. She was a tall elf in green leather armor that fit her slim figure. Her pointed ears stuck out through braided blond hair, hair that hung down to her waist. Unable to answer her question, he stared.

"Can I help you?" She repeated.

"Help," He pulled himself back together. "Right,

yes, help, you can help. Help would be good."

"Okay?" She squinted her emerald eyes together in confusion, forcing a smile to her red lips. "How can I help you?""

"Umm…one second," he wasn't sure how to remove the pizza forkhead from his inventory. To hide his ignorance, he put his hand behind his back and willed the item into his hand. He hoped it would work, and it did. The second he desired for the item to appear, it popped into existence. He held it out in front of himself. "I need you to affix this to a rod. It needs to be longer than my leg but not longer than I am tall."

She reached out with a natural grace, plucking the forkhead from his hand and examining it. "That's an interesting request. What is it for?"

"I'm a pizzaman," Pete began, "which means it is my job to make a food called pizza. When pizza cooks, it has a layer of cheese over the top. The Cheese is prone to bubble which can cause the dough to cook more in those spots. It can even burn the cheese. I am going to use the fork to reach into the oven and pop the bubbles. That way, they won't ruin the food."

"Seems simple enough," she stepped past him, patting him on the head as she did. "You be a good boy and wait here. I'll be right back."

His brain went blank for a few seconds. Wait… Did she pat his head like he was a dog? He blushed, unsure of how to respond. By the time he'd come to his senses, she was already gone. He didn't even see where she went.

"Here you go." Her voice sounded close behind him, causing him to jump. "That'll be 20 len."

Then he thought about what she had said…20 len… His eyes widened. That meant he only had 5 len left, and he still needed to get the dough. In the end, he understood he didn't have room to argue, so he made the purchase:

You have acquired a pizza fork. 5/6 ingredients needed for quest Gathering Ingredients. Gather the remaining ingredient to complete the quest.

11: Not Enough Dough for Dough

The bakery was a corner business along the road nearest the lake. Its entrance faced the massive body of water. The building was rectangle-shaped with a flat roof, its walls beige on the outside. A large, black chimney puffed up smoke in steady, circular clouds. Puff. Puff. Puff.

Through the picture frame window, Pete could see inside. An oven rested against the far wall. It boasted five broiler racks spaced at even intervals, one atop the other. Each shelf had its own glass door that allowed access to its space.

Spread across the top three racks were different varieties of bread. The most common came in the form of six-inch discs laid out on baking sheets. Along with those, he noticed some bread molds.

A waist-high counter wrapped around from the back and to the wall on the right. It formed an L shape, separating the oven from the area where displays provided customers plenty of food options: cupcakes, cakes, brownies, and of course, breads like the ones that were cooking in the oven.

The person working behind the counter—a tall elf with broad shoulders and chestnut hair—wore a white baker's hat with a matching apron. With a practiced meticulosity, he bounced from this rack to that, using tongs to pull molds and sheets from the oven. One by one, he'd remove the hot bread from the metal cookware, organizing it on the counter. Then with unmatched agility, he'd vault over the counter, gather armfuls of the bread, and organize them into their places in the sales area.

Then he'd bounce back over the counter, grab balls of uncooked dough—Pete guessed there was a bowl with the dough on a shelf under the counter, but he couldn't see from his perspective—and the baker would plop those balls onto the trays and into the molds. After loading the trays and molds, he'd sling them into the oven.

All the while, his head bobbed up and down like he was dancing. Was he listening to music? Pete thought he was. It reminded him of back at Pizza Place, how after close, the driver's and insiders would blast rap, R&B, or metal.

Pete pushed open the front door to the bakery and walked inside. The second he entered, he heard a girl's voice behind him, "welcome to Mod's Bakery. How can we help you."

"Aggh!" Pete hadn't seen anyone when he came in, so someone speaking from behind him surprised him. When he spun, he realized why he hadn't noticed them.

She was a pixie, no more than a foot tall, her long black hair pulled back into a ponytail. Behind her, black wings fluttered like a hummingbird's, causing her to hover at face level with Pete. In her right hand, she held a piece of chalk. She'd covered the black slate wall behind her with chalk-drawn pictures. The colors used were pastel: pinks, blues, yellows, greens, and oranges. One of the images reminded him of a penguin from a show he used to watch on the cartoon channel.

"Sorry," she told him. "I didn't mean to scare you. Welcome to Mod's bakery. My name is Angel. Can we help you with something?"

"Umm…yeah," Pete lifted his hat and scratched his head before returning his hat to his head. "I know this is a longshot, but I'm looking for pizza dough. Do you have any of that?"

"Perhaps," she pulled out the smallest smartphone he'd ever seen, opening it up and scrolling through apps. "If we don't have it now, I'm sure we can…" She froze, her brown eyes lifting from the phone to stare at him. "The internet says pizza dough isn't a thing. What is pizza dough?"

"It's similar to bread dough, but pizza dough has a lower ratio of water to flour, and pizza dough has oil in it." He explained.

"Sounds easy enough to make." She said. "Let me talk to Mod." She fluttered over to the baker. At the moment, he continued to work at the oven, dancing all the while. She pulled an earbud from his ear and told him, "customer has a special request."

"Special request?" He smirked: pulling the other earbud from his ear, looking at Pete. As he did this, he vaulted over the counter. Then he began in Pete's direction. "That sounds fun. My name is Mod. I'm the baker. What did you have in mind?"

Pete looked up at the baker. The elf was at least a head taller than Pete. Then Pete explained how to make pizza dough, including the ingredient ratios of his dad's secret recipe. "After you make it, you divide it into doughballs. The larger the doughball, the bigger the pizza, but they need to be fist-sized. I need at least one of those."

"What do you do with the dough after you divide it into the doughballs?" Mod asked.

Pete answered, "From there, you slap and pull the ball until it is a thin disc. You leave an elevated border on the disc. The border should be about as big as the piece of chalk that Angel is holding."

"Why do you have an elevated border?" Mod seemed excited like a child getting a new toy on Christmas. In a way, it made sense. After making the same bread and dessert recipes, it must be nice to find something new to make.

Pete replied. "The borders hold in a tomato sauce, melted cheese, and any other ingredients you put on the dough. We call the things you put on it toppings. After you get the pizza with all the toppings you want, you bake it."

"And after you bake it?" Mod continued to ask questions.

LEGEND

"After," Pete willed the pizza cutter to his hand, "you cut it into triangular pieces with this."

"Like a pie?" Angel entered the conversation.

"Exactly," Pete told her.

"Swag…" The pixie smiled, pointing her finger to the side. Then she flew back to the wall and continued to draw on it.

"How much will dough cost?" Pete asked.

"Based on what you told me," Mod scratched his chin, considering, "ten len. It will be more than normal bread because it is a special request, and it will take away from my usual work." Ten len? Pete hung his head; he only had five left. Upon seeing this, Mod added. "Or I can do it for free. As long as you show us how to make it. We can use my ovens. Also, once you've made it, you have to share."

That was an offer that Pete couldn't refuse.

Josh Walker

12: I Am a Proficient Slapper

You have acquired a pizza dough. 6/6 ingredients needed for quest Gathering Ingredients. You have gathered all the ingredients. To complete the quest, put the ingredients together, bake them, and create the first pizza in Round!

Pete poured a small pile of flour onto the counter. Then he dropped the doughball into the flour. From there, he began to slap, shape, and stretch the dough. With each movement, he seemed to gain proficiency in slapping.

You gained .2 slapping proficiency.

You gained .1 slapping proficiency.

You gained .3 slapping proficiency.

By the time he finished shaping the first doughball into a crust, he had gained at least five full proficiency points. To balance and stretch the crust, he tossed it into the air, spinning it.

You gained 1 tossing proficiency.

"Mod," he asked, "do you have a cooking screen or stone about this size?"

The cook hurried to a spot near the oven, grabbing a stack of cooking screens, and setting them next to Pete.

Pete slid the first one to the counter with his elbow. It rolled on its edges like a spinning quarter before settling even with the flat surface. At that point, Pete flopped the crust atop the screen. He evened the edges of the screen with those of the dough. Then Pete moved to the next doughball.

What was strange was how each full point seemed to make slapping the dough easier. Within thirty seconds, he had made another two crusts. With those pizzas, he gained another five to ten proficiency points.

Mod the baker had enough dough for three or four more pizzas. As such, Pete decided to let Mod practice making the dough for himself. In the meantime, Pete summoned three of the tomatoes from his inventory. After, he asked Angel for a knife, eggbeater, peeler, and bowl.

She pointed to a space under the counter, "there is a steel mixing bowl down there. There are a knife and peeler in the drawer to your right."

"Thanks," Pete grabbed the cookware, peeled his tomatoes, cut them into a puree, and dropped them into a mixing bowl. Pete could have made pizza sauce without anything other than the tomatoes. Yet, he knew a recipe that would make it better. For said recipe, he requested those ingredients: olive oil, sugar, butter, salt, oregano, basil, thyme, garlic powder, and crushed peppers. Other than the peppers, Mod had everything available in his bakery.

Pete finished the sauce as Mod finished the last crust. They used a ladle to scoop the sauce onto each crust. From there, they spread an even layer of the red paste over the crust. Then they grated cheese over the top. All the while, Mod and Angel watched with fascination. "We won't be able to eat all this pizza on our own. Do either of you know people who you want to share it with?"

Without answering, Angel sped to the door before looking at Mod. "Quick, I need to get the triplets."

"Right," Mod agreed, moving to the door. "The triplets will love it. Can you stop by the mayor and Lilly, too? We should invite them." Mod reached the door and pushed it open.

"Bet," Angel sped outside.

Through the open door, Pete noticed the sun had begun to go down. He didn't realize how late it had gotten. When Max the cat teleported him to Greenlake, it must have been earlier in the afternoon. Pete thought it had been morning. Regardless of the time, Pete felt hunger cramps beginning to torment him. Good thing he'd have pizza soon. He told Mod. "We should put those pizzas in the oven."

Mod agreed, and one by one, they loaded the pizzas onto the oven racks. Mod asked. "When will they finish cooking?"

"If the ovens are the same temperature as the ones I use back home, it should be eight to ten minutes. We will need to keep an eye on them to see when the crust begins to brown. Also..." Pete summoned the pizza fork to his hand. "We will need to use this to pop any cheese bubbles, so everything bakes how we want it to."

The eight minutes dragged by but popping the rogue cheese bubble kept Pete and Mod occupied. Then, when the pizzas began to look ready, Pete summoned his peel, using its broad metal head to pull a pizza from the oven. Once out, he set the pizza on the counter.

He summoned his cutter to his hand and ran the wheel across the pizza four times, creating eight slices. He tried to keep them the same size. A series of prompts appeared:

Congratulations. You have completed the quest Gathering Ingredients. Now, the world of Round will know you as the inventor of pizza. Also, Pizzamandom is a word. Don't think it isn't.

Did the prompt respond to his doubt about its use of the word from before? Pete still didn't think that was a real word. Two more prompts appeared:

You gained 1 point pizza cutter proficiency.

You received 250 experience points.
Congratulations! You gained a level!

You earned 200 len.

You completed a job-related quest. You receive 3 bonus job points.

Before Pete closed the prompts, he took a quick glance at his status screen. He smiled when he saw his high slapping proficiency. Then he closed the prompts, saying. "The pizza is ready. Do you have a spatula or something we can use to lift the slices onto plates?"

"I do," Mod smiled, pulling a triangular-shaped spatula—one used for slices of pie—from the drawer. Consequently, it was the same drawer that held the peel. He handed the spatula to Pete. "I'll grab some plates, too...and stools, so people have places to sit. Company should be arriving soon."

"Right," Pete nodded. "Thanks, Mod." As he said the name, he realized he'd never met someone named Mod before. "Hey, Mod. Do you mind if I ask a question?"

"Go ahead."

"Where does the name Mod come from?"

"People who believe in literal, sentient moderators call themselves mods. It's a type of religion." He explained, bringing back a stack of plates, taking the one off the top of the pile, setting it next to the pizza. "My parents were religious."

"That makes sense." Pete likened it to someone

whose parents name them Christian back on earth. "Here is a slice for you." Pete used the spatula to lift a slice onto Mod's plate. As he lifted the cheese stretched and Mod's eyes widened with anticipation. "While you try that, I'm going to pull the other pizzas from the oven."

One by one, Pete removed the cheese pizzas, setting them side by side on the counter. After, he turned to Mod who was already serving himself a second slice, an enormous smile on his face. Mod finished another slice and said, "this is amazing."

"Everyone loves pizza," Pete nodded his agreement.

13: Pixies Love Pizza

Angel the pixie zipped around town with a simple message. "Pete the pizzaman made pizza. Come try it." She told the triplets; she told the mayor; she told Nick the guard; she told Lilly... Then she told every pixie in town. Then the mayor, Lilly, the triplets, and the rest of the pixies made their way to the bakery to try the new food.

*   *   *

Back in the store, Pete and Mod ate. They left a window cracked open for when Angel returned, but Angel wasn't the first pixie to arrive. Instead, a pixie—she was shorter than Angel by at least an inch or two—fluttered inside. She hesitated, looking left and right. Then she locked her eyes on Mod, and her teal wings carried her toward him.

Waist-length hair flowed behind her as she flew. She wore black tights. Two sets of neon lines crisscrossed up and down each leg. Her shirt was bright yellow. On its center, a mustached face smiled and winked.

Following close behind her, two more pixies entered through the window. In the back, their hair was short, cut at the nape. In front, bangs hung down to their eyes. On the sides, messy hair covered their ears. One pixie had blue wings and wore a white t-shirt. Black lines formed a face in the center of the shirt. It reminded Pete of a laughing emojie.

The third pixie had red wings. The wings zig zagged on the edges, tapering toward the center like a tornado. He wore a red shirt with a tornado on it.

DAB!

When the trio approached, Pete realized they must be the triplets. They had the same chestnut hair, the same green eyes. Their olive-shaped faces, pink lips, and button noses made it hard to tell them apart.

When they reached Mod, they landed on the counter next to him. The one with long hair touched the tip of her pointer fingers together and spoke. "Hi, Mod. We heard you have Pete's za. Angel said we should come try it. What is za?"

"It's called pizza, P-I-Z-Z-A." Mod grinned, spelling it out. "And it is delicious. Pete is the name of the person who invented it. Let me introduce you." Mod nodded at Pete. "This is Pete the pizzaman."

Pete waved at the triplets.

"Hi, Pete." The green-winged pixie with long hair waved back. "My name is Hope. These two are my brothers. This is Skye." She looked at the one with the white emoji shirt, and he waved. Then she looked at her other brother. "This is Tornado."

"Tornado," Tornado said, jumping in the air and spinning in a few circles before landing back on the counter.

"Nice to meet you," Pete said. "Are you ready to try pizza?"

"Before I answer that," She examined the slice on Pete's plate and then looked back to the slice in Mod's hand. "I had a question about pizza."

"What is your question?" Pete wondered.

"Does it have bacon in it?" Her question seemed hopeful.

"It can have bacon," Pete replied. "Unfortunately, this pizza does not."

"That's too bad," the pixie hung her head.

Pete smiled, observing. "I bet you are friends with Nick the guard, aren't you?"

"How'd you know?" She looked up at him.

"Lucky guess," Pete grinned, standing up. Then

he used his pizza cutter to prepare and plate three smaller slices for the trio.

When he set it down in front of them, Tornado began eating without hesitation. Hope took a cautious first bite. Then she smiled and continued to eat.

Skye was more cautious, poking and prodding the strange new cuisine. "Are you sure it's food?" He went from wrinkling his forehead, to widening his eyes, to wrinkling his nose, to raising an eyebrow, to wrinkling a forehead again.

Pete nodded that he was sure it was food.

"But are you sure?" This time Skye looked him straight in the eye. "You wouldn't lie to a pixie…would you?"

"Try it." Pete encouraged.

Skye stared Pete straight in the eyes for a few more seconds before saying. "Okay, I'll try it." With caution, he lifted the small piece of pizza to his mouth. Then he bit off a piece and chewed with a slow caution. As he swallowed, he smiled ear to ear, and with the pizza still in hand, he dabbed with his left arm out and his right arm in. Then he dabbed to the other side. Then he kept eating.

At that moment, the mayor pushed open the front door. She seemed to speed walk, but after a few steps into the bakery, she froze in place, lifting her head and sniffing the air. Her eyes widened in anticipation. "What is that smell? It is wonderful. Is that smell pizza?"

"Sure is," Pete prepared the mayor a slice and handed it to her on a plate. "We have lots of pizza and not enough people to eat it, so have as much as you want."

After she ate her first bite, she declared. "This is good. This is real good. This is wonderful. Are you sure I can have as much as I want? You promise? No backsies!"

"I promise." Pete nodded, smiling. One of his favorite things was watching people try something for the first time. He especially liked watching movies with people that hadn't seen the movie. He enjoyed seeing how they reacted to each scene. He wondered if Round had movies and television? If not, he'd have to invent them later. That day, he'd already invented pizza, and that was enough.

Nick the guard was the next to arrive. As he entered the door, he held up a cloth bag that seemed wet with grease. "I brought bacon." Pete noticed Hope's eyes light up. "I hope this is as good as you say."

Pete handed him a plate with a slice. "Try for yourself."

Nick pulled a small piece of cooked bacon from his bag and began to break it into bits over his pizza slice. When Hope asked for some, he shared with her, breaking bits of bacon over her slice, too. After Nick began to eat, he said. "That isn't bad, son. I can't wait to try the one with all the meats. Good work."

A few minutes later, Angel returned, "The others should be here soon." Then her eyes took in the room. She saw everyone sitting, the triplets on the counter, the mayor, Pete, Nick, and Mod on stools. Each person had a smile on their face.

Pete looked at her and handed her a small piece of pizza. "Try some."

After she took her first bit, her eyes widened. "Epic!" When she said the word, she accented and extended the 'i' sound to make it last a few seconds.

Pete couldn't understand why she spoke with slang from the 2020s, but he appreciated it. It reminded him of his childhood when all the cool kids talked like that.

Minutes later, more pixies showed up. There were too many to count, and Pete struggled to keep up with all their names. Even so, he realized he'd have time to learn their names. The important thing was that each of them got enough pizza. To ensure they did, he remained attentive. When they finished a slice. They received a new one; they always had a slice on their tiny, pixie sized plates. As he served the last slice of pizza that he and Mod had made, Pete came to a realization. Pixies love pizza.

As the day came to a close, and people and pixies returned to their homes, Pete realized something. He didn't have a home. His concern must have shown because Mod asked him, "is something wrong?"

"Thinking," Pete explained. "I'm not sure where I'm going to stay the night. Is there an inn nearby?"

"Why do you need an inn?" Mod asked.

Pete didn't understand the implication of Mod's question because he was too busy checking his inventory sheet to see his len. "How much does a night in an inn cost? Under 205 len?"

"Why do you need an inn?" Mod repeated. "I stay here. I have an extra room. I used to rent it out...haven't had a tenant in years. You can have it."

At that point, Pete understood. "You want to rent it to me?"

"Or you can work for me," Mod explained. "With your pizza, I'll more than recoup the cost of letting you stay here for free. Consider this a job offer."

Pete continued to review his inventory sheet. He had seven tomatoes and two blocks of cheese. "That would be great, but I only have two blocks of cheese left. I used almost half my tomatoes. We will need more ingredients."

"Well, I can use the cheese and dough I have here. Also, I know of three other nightshade spawn points. They are deeper into the forest, but not too deep. You can farm tomatoes from them.

"You are on to something with this pizza stuff. If

you work for me, we can make this bakery world famous. What do you say? Why don't you go farm some
more tomatoes tomorrow, come back here, and we can
begin this venture together?" A mission prompt appeared:

You have been offered the quest, "Job Offer." Completion reward: 300 len, 350 experience points. Do you
accept the quest?

Pete blinked away the prompt. "Mod, I'll take
you up on that. Thank you for the opportunity."

You have accepted the quest, "Job Offer." Farm tomatoes at all three nightshade terror spawn points and es-
tablish the first pizzeria in Round.

Josh Walker

14: Zoey's Drive Home

Every Saturday, Zoey would text Pete to talk about the Isekai they watched the night before. After their discussion, they'd spend the afternoon playing an MMO on the same server. Pete liked to handle DPS while Zoey enjoyed playing the tank. Of course, they were in the same guild. So they had other DPS, buffers, debuffers, and healers to provide them plenty of support. After an afternoon of raids, Pete and Zoey would work the same closing shift at Pizza Place.

Pete didn't do any of those things. He didn't answer any of her texts. He didn't log on for gaming. He didn't show up for his work shift. It wasn't like him, and she didn't understand it. Was he okay? In the last two years, he hadn't missed a single day. He never called out. He was the responsible type. She was worried.

After closing the store by herself, she decided to sit in her car for a few minutes and check his online status... He hadn't made any posts. Had anyone seen him after they closed together the night before? Did something happen to him, and he felt like dealing with it himself? If she didn't hear from him soon, she decided to go to the police and report him missing.

She sighed and shook her head, telling herself. "You're going to drive yourself crazy if you keep this up. I'm sure he's fine." She put her key in the ignition and turned. Then she began the ride home.

That night, she'd delivered pizza to over twenty different addresses. Sometimes it took her fifteen minutes to get to a place. Sometimes it took her forty-five minutes. Under normal circumstances, the ride home was less than either of those times. But that night, the drive home seemed so much longer. She couldn't stop worrying. "Pete, where are you?" She asked aloud, turning onto a street that brought her into the neighborhood where she lived.

A cat ran in front of her car, and she slammed on her brakes. The worn pads squeezed against the rotors, and the car screeched to a stop. *That was a close one,* she thought, watching as a woman chased close behind the cat.

The woman wore a white nightgown. Such vestment caused Zoey to think that the woman hadn't planned to be chasing a cat through the streets at two in the morning. The frilly sleeping garb looked impossible to move in. It impressed Zoey how the woman moved as fast as she did.

Zoey's eyes watched as the woman reached the other side of the street and closed on the cat. When it seemed the woman was about to grab her pet—Zoey assumed it was her pet, anyway—the cat slipped away and sped up a tall tree.

Zoey sighed and whispered to herself, "There is no way anyone can climb wearing that gown. I better help out." She rolled her car to the curb before putting it in park, turning off the engine, and turning off the ignition.

Before she opened the car door, she checked for traffic. It wasn't that she expected any on a quiet residential street, not at that time of night. Yet, a person can never be too careful.

When no one was coming, she pushed the door open and hurried out.

Then she realized something. What if the whole thing was a setup? She'd heard stories of people lying down on the side of the road, pretending to be in trouble. When a driver stops to help them, lots of other people jump out of bushes and ambush the driver. Those people try to steal the car or hurt the driver.

At the thought of this, Zoey's heart beat a little bit faster.

Though, if someone did want to start something with her, she knew how to take care of herself. Years of

SCA, kendo, jiujitsu, boxing, and karate could vouch for that. She had a black belt in three of those. Not to mention, she had a can of pepper spray on her key chain.

When she looked around, she calmed. There weren't many bushes to hide behind; the street's only suitable cover came in the form of a few tall elms and some pine trees. "It's only a woman who needs some help chasing her pet cat." Zoey convinced herself and jogged across the street, keeping her guard up all the same. "Hey," She spoke with a louder voice than usual, so the woman could hear her, but Zoey was careful not to shout. "Do you need any help?"

The woman turned her head to look at Zoey, and the woman was smiling. This wasn't a smile of relief.

Instead, the smile the woman offered was toothy, extending ear to ear. It seemed...Zoey wasn't sure if predatory was the right word, but she felt like prey. A chill ran down her spine, and she shivered. Speaking of predators...the woman's smile exposed her teeth. The sharpness of her canines seemed abnormal. How did someone get their teeth so sharp? Did she file them?

"Thank goodness," the woman spoke with a voice that seemed forced. It reminded Zoey of her high school nemesis when her nemesis got the lead in the annual high school play. Fifteen was her name, and she could not act.

The sharp-toothed woman in a gown...was she acting? Was she a bad actress like Kim? That didn't make any sense. How would she train a cat to run into a tree? Zoey guessed the girl was nervous. That had to be why she seemed off. "Max always runs away like this. I can't get up there in this gown. Do you think you can get him down?"

"Sure thing," Zoey nodded, examining the tree for a way to climb it.

15: Job Offer

Pete opened his job skills screen. He had five points to allocate. As he squinted his eyes and examined the screen, he felt torn. Should he pump three points into steel hands? It would allow him to slap with twice the proficiency for a limited amount of time. His other choice was using all five points into strong fire.

In the end, he went with his gut and chose to do steel hands. This opened up three new abilities: strong steel hands, oven survival, and strong heat resist. He glanced at them.

Strong steel hands increased his slapping proficiency even further than its standard version. Oven Survival provided 100% burn resistance to pans, allowing a person to remove pans from the oven with their bare hands. Strong Heat Resist offered a 40% resistance to the heat, including heat-based attacks like fire.

As it was, Pete didn't have enough job points to unlock anything else, so he closed the menu. With that done, he pushed off his blanket, rolled off the mattress where he slept, and began to dress.

At that point, he remembered the hole in his shirt. If he'd been back on Earth, his manager would have made him change it...or Zoey would have...or his mom would have...whichever of them saw it first. For the time, he couldn't change his shirt...it was the only one he had. Sooner rather than later, he'd need to get a replacement, but he wasn't sure what he wanted as a replacement. He supposed he could repair it in the meantime. Rather, the tailor could repair it. Later, Pete would have to check with them.

Another thing he hadn't figured out was how to bathe. He felt weird asking Mod about a bathtub. What if that world didn't have bathtubs? What if they didn't have showers? What if they didn't bathe at all? Did people not stink there? Pete smelled under his arm, causing him to wrinkle his nose and draw back. Did Round have deodorant?

If worse came to worse, he'd have to commission a swimsuit with one of the artisans in town and use the lake for a bath. He'd figure that out later, though. Since he had to go hunting nightshade terrors at their various spawn points, he was going to work up a sweat, anyway. It didn't make sense to clean up before that.

When he exited the bedroom in the back of the bakery, Mod was already awake, baking what looked like deserts. While still going through his routines, Mod asked. "Did you sleep well?"

"I did." Pete nodded. "Thank you again."

"No problem."

From there, the two enjoyed a few comfortable seconds of silence. Then Pete said. "I'm going to farm those tomatoes."

"I'll see you when you get back. Stay safe." Mod pulled a pie from the oven setting it on the counter, and Pete continued out the bakery's front door.

No sooner had he stepped outside when a dust devil kicked up dirt near his feet. Chasing behind the dust devil was the pixie named Tornado. His two siblings watched from a nearby corner, eyes wide with surprise.

When Tornado caught up to the wind phenomenon, he jumped, hurling his body into it and yelling, "tornado." It caught his wings, spinning him before flinging him into the air. His wings fluttered as the dizzy child bobbed back and forth in the air before touching back down to earth. He laughed all the while. His two siblings joined him in his laughter.

Pete smiled and continued through town, passing by people. That early in the morning, he guessed most were on their way to work or school. When he reached the city gate, he came across Nick the guard.

"Good morning, son," Nick nodded at Pete. "That was good pizza last night. When do you think you will have one with all the meats?"

"Soon," Pete answered. "I'm starting to figure out how things work around here. If we're lucky, I'll have an all the meats pizza for you soon. When I make it will depend on what Mod can find in the market. Also, it depends on how many more tomatoes I can farm today."

A wrinkle of concern creased Nick's forehead. "Are you going up the mountain path into the forest again?"

"That's the plan," Pete confessed, asking. "Should I not do that? Am I not allowed to farm tomatoes like that? I'm sorry if it is a silly question. I'm trying to learn and remember all the rules in Round."

"I understand." Nick shook his head, no. "But it isn't anything like that. We've recently had reports of thieves in the woods. So far, they've stuck to doing their work at night, ambushing unsuspecting travelers. You should be fine but be careful."

Pete nodded his understanding. "If they attack, am I allowed to defend myself?"

"You can defend yourself against any impending attacks. It will not violate any local laws; it will not violate any of the laws of the moderators." Nick explained.

"Good to know," Pete told him. "Thanks for looking out, Nick."

"Looking out?" Nick cocked his head to the side. It was his way of asking what the phrase meant.

"It means taking care of someone," Pete told him.

"Oh," Nick resumed a normal posture and smiled. "I get it. It is short for looking out for someone. That is good. Young people speak amuses me. Thank you for looking out and keeping me entertained, Son."

"Anytime," Pete told him. "I'll catch you later."

"I doubt you could catch me." The guard told the pizzaman. "My agility rating is very high."

"Alright then, I'll talk to you later. Have a great day." Pete continued past the gate, through the fields, and to the muddy path. Then he pressed up the muddy path into the forested mountains.

Unlike the last time he'd fought the plants, he had to find his own way to the nightshade terror spawn points. He wondered if there is a map prompt that could guide him to them… Or a waypoint arrow. When he thought about a map, one appeared.

It was a small circle in the top right of his vision. He could zoom in, zoom out, and reorient it with a thought. He could also change the units of measurement it used. He changed the unit to miles.

Three inverted triangles pointed to different locations on the map. When he looked at the triangles, the quest name, 'Job Offer,' appeared over them. "Those have got to be the three respawn points." He said, realizing they were about a mile further in than where he'd fought the other plants.

Landmarks were also marked out on the map, including one called the Rock Table. From what he could tell, it was the rocky outcropping at the top of the cliff face. If that were the case, it would provide a fantastic view of the town. Pete decided he had time for the detour.

He continued up the trail, examining the other symbols on the map. One of the symbols was a yellow circle with some type of bison skull inside it. Of all the symbols, it was the only one that moved, but it seemed to remain within the bounds of the forest far to the north. In relation to the symbol, Pete couldn't get any identifying notifications to pop up. Nonetheless, he guessed it was a notorious monster.

Pete climbed the path up the mountain, through

the trees, following it as it curved from north to west. When Rock Table was straight south of him, he broke away from the path. Two minutes later, he came to the outcropping. True to its name, it was flat, like a large, gray, stone table. Pete walked onto it and took in the view.

From the high vantage point, he could see the entire town of Greenlake. It rested on the southern bank of the lake. Due to the body of water's enormous size, Pete could not see to its other side.

Green, hilly fields extended as far as he could see to the west. To the east, those hills ended in mountains, including the volcano he had noticed before.

In the country, he noticed the occasional house. They looked like tiny white boxes. Some had red barns next to them.

Back home, he'd never witnessed so many beautiful colors mixed together in a natural setting. The green of the vegetation contrasted with the deep blue of the lake. The volcano, purple mountains, and their white snowcaps blended with a cerulean sky.

If he had the time for it, Pete would have stayed there all day, but he knew he didn't. Instead, he returned to the path, continuing through the forest until he reached the first spawn point.

As he arrived, he examined the plant monsters. There were five of them, each of them level one. Where his first encounter with the monsters was less than ideal, he felt more confident this time. So he jumped straight in. One slap. Two. Three. Four. Five. After five slaps, there were five dead plants. One of the plants did manage to scratch him, though... It caused 2 HP of damage.

Prompts indicated he gained twenty to thirty experience points per creature. Also, he received twelve more tomato plants. Fighting the monsters reminded him of the beginning of a JRPG. When he played those games, one of his favorite things to do was level up on the weak monsters at the beginning of the game. When he was twenty to thirty levels higher than everything in an area, he'd move on.

This strategy made the games take longer to get through, but he never had to worry about getting frustrated at a boss battle. In Round, a similar approach seemed appropriate. Instead of frustration, he could avoid death by power leveling. Though, he wasn't sure if power leveling was against the rules of the moderators.

A bush rustled to his left, pulling him away from his prompts. When he investigated, he didn't see anyone, but he noticed some footprints in the mud. They seemed human-shaped, bigger than a pixie's but smaller than a regular-sized person's. Had someone been watching him? He looked around. When he didn't see anyone, he moved on to the next spawn point.

The area held six nightshade terrors, five level ones, and a level two. He used his new skill steel hands, doubling his slapping proficiency. This provided a significant increase to his attack. Then he targeted the level two monster. The attack caused the monster three hundred HP of damage. After, he made quick work of the other plants.

In the end, he gained two-hundred-three more experience and added sixteen tomatoes to his inventory. After the battle, he received the standard proficiency prompts, too. When his slapping proficiency rose over forty, he earned a new prompt:

You have learned slapping skill Slap'm Silly. Use Slap'm Silly to render an opponent unconscious without depleting their HP.

Nightshade Terror
Level 3

That skill is terrific, Pete thought. It would be nice to be able to slap things without having to worry about killing them. And if he ever had a difficult time falling asleep, he could use the skill on himself.

Bushes near him rustled again, and he pulled away from the prompts.

Near the bush, he found the same, small footprints. He took some time to search the area, but he couldn't follow the tracks in any specific direction. So he sighed, decided not to worry about the footprints, and moved to the third spawn area.

It only had two of the creatures, a level one and a level three. Level three? Pete worried as he looked at the beast. It was massive, at least a head taller than Pete. It had countless fingers and vines sprouting from its hands and body.

Could he win against a level three? Pete pulled up his HP. He still had 79/84. He thought he could take them, but he needed to be careful. If things got out of hand, he needed to be able to run. Should he target the level one monster first or the level three?

He made his decision and leaped into action, slapping across the weaker creature. It dropped, becoming a lifeless pile of vines. As he spun to face the larger monster, he activated Steel Hands. Yet before he could swing, it cut across his shoulder, tearing a new hole into his pizza uniform. Then the attack cut through his skin.

After reading a prompt that he had received 12 HP of damage, Pete answered the creature's attack. As the other nightshade terrors had died in one slap. This level three monster did not...so Pete slapped it again. The second slap did the trick, causing the plant to fall. Prompts appeared. One of them read:

Congratulations! You gained a level!

Pete threw his hands up and shouted, "WOOOOOT!"

A disturbing rumble answered his wooting. It came from nearby trees. He wondered if making loud sounds in the forest was a mistake. A gigantic turkey emerged from behind a tree, running straight at him. At that moment, he knew it was a mistake to make loud noises in a forest.

The words above the turkey identified it as The Turkey Titan. It was level twelve, way too strong for Pete to fight, so he turned and ran. While he escaped, he jumped over branches and juked around trees. Moments later, he reached the muddy path and followed it all the way to Greenlake.

When he finally turned around, he realized the turkey...was nowhere in sight. It hadn't followed him. As he panted to catch his breath, he realized one other thing. Even though there was no stamina bar, he could still get tired.

16: Grand Opening

When Pete entered the bakery, Mod's eyes fell on him, blinking twice before Mod asked. "You okay?"

Pete looked down at his torn shirt. The holes made him feel uncomfortable, and he knew he'd need to replace the shirt as soon as possible. After examining the rips, he answered. "You don't know the half of it. There was a giant turkey."

"Turkey Titan?" Mod smiled. "Most people know to look for notorious monsters on their map and avoid them. You got close enough to see it?"

"It snuck up on me when I was fighting the plants," Pete explained.

"Well, at least you're okay. Did you get the tomatoes?" Mod's voice was hopeful.

"I have enough to get us through the week until the other plants respawn. I don't think we'll ever have a supply problem."

"Great," Mod smiled. "Then let's get to work."

Usual bread and pastry customers continued to come in. Between helping the customers, Mod and Pete prepared sauce, grated cheese, and made doughballs. As they finished their prep work, Angel flew through one of the windows. "Here and ready to work," her eyes widened when she saw the pizza dough, cheese, and sauce. "We get pizza again?"

"We're going to try to sell them today." Mod nodded.

"Epic." Angel landed on the counter. "You want me to let everyone know?"

"Sure," Mod agreed. "That would be great."

"On it." Angel flew back out the window. Pete and Mod could hear her shouting in the distance. "Pizza! Come try pizza! It's the best food in Round! Invented right here in Greenlake."

Over the next few hours, people came in, some

ordering pizza, some ordering bread, pie, or cake. Interacting with the customers reminded Pete of a late shift at Pizza Place.

Pete enjoyed interacting with customers. It was one of his favorite parts of the job. Each person with whom he spoke had a unique story. He loved to learn about their interests and aspirations.

The Carpenter elf was one of those customers. The night before, Pete had learned her name was Lilly. When she entered the store, she asked. "Is Mod here? I wanted to talk with him."

"Yeah, I'll go grab him," Pete told her.

Mod came and spoke with Lilly for a few minutes. Pete kept his distance as to not intrude on what could be a private conversation.

As Pete watched Mod interact with Lilly, it reminded him of his relationship with Zoey. The pair seemed comfortable together. When the thought of Zoey entered his mind, Pete felt nostalgic. Thoughts of Zoey became thoughts of his family. He hoped he'd be able to return home sooner rather than later.

Max the cat had told Pete that the only way to return home was to save Round. Pete wasn't sure he could do that. He didn't even know what Round needed saving from. During his time in Greenlake, everything seemed okay. The citizens weren't threatened by some great evil.

Even if there was an identifiable threat to Round, Pete wouldn't be able to face it. After all, a turkey had caused Pete to flee for his life. If he couldn't defeat a turkey, how could he defeat something strong enough to dictate the fate of an entire world?

He sighed. For the time, all he could do was try to get stronger. Once he had another twenty or thirty levels under his belt, would he be strong enough to leave Greenlake? Then he could learn more about the world. Still, he doubted he'd ever be strong enough to be its savior.

As Lilly the carpenter left, Pete moved next to Mod. "She might like you. You should ask for the number of her communication box."

Mod turned to Pete, blinking three times before answering. "I already have her number. She's my sister."

"Oh…" Pete hung his head. "Nevermind then. Pretend I didn't say anything." Then Pete changed the topic. "So do you think you'll be able to keep up with all the pizza orders? Are we going to run out of any supplies?"

"I can get the cheese and dough without difficulty. The sauce relies on your tomatoes, but since one sauce bucket can make multiple pizzas, we should be good. If I had to, I could import tomatoes from nearby towns, too. They are more common in other parts."

"Cool," Pete said, moving to pull some pizzas from the oven. As he cut them into slices, prompts appeared:

You received 2 to pizza cutter proficiency.

You received 1.5 to pizza cutter proficiency.

You received 1 to pizza cutter proficiency.

Each time he used the peel, prompts indicated his peel skill level increased, too. At Pizza Place, he'd always joked about using pizza peels as shields. If his proficiency raised enough, he could use it as a shield. That would be awesome. He would be a pizza knight.

And he continued to cut the pizza's increasing his cutting proficiency. If he raised his cutter skill enough, he wondered if he could fight with them. Would it be a viable option? Then he wouldn't have to slap everything.

As the night went on, word of pizzas at the bakery spread. Pete and Mod found themselves unprepared to deal with the influx of customers. They'd give one a pizza, three more customers would show up. They'd help the three, and they'd have ten more customers. After they helped those ten, the line was out the door.

Angel came zipping back through the door. "I told everyone."

"We can see that," Mod told her while working at the oven to put pizzas in and take them out. "Can you help Pete to take some orders?"

"Sure thing, bossman." She fluttered next to Pete. "I can help the next customer over here."

It was late at night before they finished helping the last customer. At which point, Pete sat on the floor and slumped with his back against the counter. "That was busy."

"I agree," Angel told him, lying face first, exhausted on the countertop.

Mod shook his head, "We are going to need more help. Angel, how many of your pixie friends still need jobs?"

17: They Think I Invented Food Delivery

One way or another, Pete knew Mod would need more help. Hiring more pixies seemed like an excellent way to streamline services. It would help the customers would get their food faster. Sure, those customers were happy with the new food. Even so, if they had to wait thirty minutes or more every time they ordered, they'd get grumpy with the service. Mod and his place needed to streamline how they provided the service.

"How about we take orders by communication box?" Pete suggested. "After we take a person's order, we can deliver it to people in their own homes."

"Deliver food?" Angel raised an eyebrow. "Is that a thing? That would be amazing to call and have dinner come to you."

"Where I am from," Pete explained. "You can order almost any food you want and have it delivered to your house. Hamburgers, French fries, pizza, sandwiches, Chinese food, anything."

"I don't know what those are." Angel squinted her eyes together. "But it sounds cool."

Mod entered the conversation. "I like the idea of pizza delivery. I could also deliver my other baked goods. Pete, do you think you'd be able to track the orders and get people the food they wanted to their houses?"

"That was my job back home," Pete replied. "I wasn't in the pizza store that much. I focused on deliveries. Some nights, I'd do thirty or forty deliveries. In a town the size of Greenlake, delivery should be a piece of cake."

"Piece of cake?" Mod asked.

"It's a saying," Pete explained. "It means it will be easy."

"Ah, I see. That saying doesn't make sense." Mod said. After a few seconds of pause, he continued, "I have one other thing I wanted to talk about."

"What's that?" Pete asked.

"We need to give the store a new name, and we need to give you a job title." Mod scratched his temple with his finger. "I was thinking of calling it M and P's Pizzeria and Baked Goods."

"That works for me," Pete agreed. "I like it."

"Great," Mod smiled, "and what job title should we give you?"

"Pizza Delivery Driver?" Pete asked.

"Driver?" Angel pointed out. "You don't have a vehicle. What will you be driving."

"That's a fair point," Pete agreed. "You could call me a pizza delivery specialist?"

"That works," Mod and Angel answered in unison."

A prompt appeared:

You have completed the quest Job Offer.

You received 300 len. You received 350 experience points.

Pete closed the prompts, saying. "We'll need uni-forms, too."

"Right," Mod agreed. "I'd prefer you to have something more durable than cloth. It will prevent the issue you have with your current uniform."

An uncomfortable Pete answered, "right, that might be a good idea. You think your sister Lilly could come up with something?"

Mod considered Pete's words before answering. "I don't think so. You might want to try the tailor. They know some leatherwork, too. Even so, cloth uniforms should be enough for the Pixies. Hope, I'll let you come up with a design for them."

"You got it," the pixie smiled. "I have so many ideas for them. I'll use Pete's current uniform as a pattern. You're going to love it."

For a few more moments, they discussed the logistics of how a pizza delivery place needs to operate, and how they would implement the new pixie staff. Then Pete retreated to his bedroom.

The night before, he didn't have much time to look at the room, so he decided to take a closer look at it. The mattress was similar to what he had back home. Though, instead of springs, feathers and hay seemed to fill it. A similar filling was in his pillow. It reminded him of a pillow his grandma used to own.

A chest of drawers pushed up against the north wall, the bed laid out in the southeast corner. A mirror hung on the west wall. A small window was on the east wall.

Pete rested in bed, considering everything he'd been through over the last two days: the cat in the tree, the conversation in the booth with the cat named Max, meeting Nick the guard, and the mayor who was a gnome.

He smiled as he remembered how his conversation with the mayor had gone. Then he worried, what if he hadn't been able to ask someone how to close his prompts? What if he still didn't know how to close them? He shuddered at the thought.

He remembered hunting the tomato plants, meeting Mod, running from the turkey, and the busy day at Mod's Bakery... It used to be Mod's Bakery, anyway. In all his life, Pete wasn't sure he'd ever been through so much.

With all that, he still hadn't taken a bath. He planned to make it a priority for the next day. Even if he had to sneak to the lake in the morning, he'd do it. No one had mentioned his smell to him yet. But he was sure they would if he went any longer without taking care of basic hygiene. That reminded him, he'd also have to ask about how people brushed their teeth in Round.

Pete pulled out his cellphone; its battery had dipped to two percent. He'd also have to go to the nearest Communication Box retailer and see about getting a plan for his device. He hoped he wouldn't have to buy a new phone altogether. Either way, he would need to come up with a way to charge his phone. He hoped they'd have a wireless charger, so he wouldn't have to match his port to anything specific.

Either way, he understood those were all things to do in the morning. In the meantime, he only had one objective. He needed to rest, but he had one more thing to do before he went to bed. He pulled up his status page:

NAME: Pete   **RACE:** Human   **JOB:** Pizzaman

LEVEL 5

HP: 104/104
MP: 7/7

STR: 19
DEX: 14
VIT: 18
INT: 14
SPR: 9
AGI: 13

ALIGNMENT: Lawful Good
RELIGION: Christian
LANGUAGES: English,
                Spanish,
                Common
GENDER: Male
HEIGHT: 5'8
WEIGHT: 145 lbs
AGE: 20
EYES: Blue
Hair: Blond

LEFT ARM: Unequipped
RIGHT ARM: Unequipped
HEAD: Pizza Place Hat
BODY: Torn Pizza Place Polo
LEGS: Black Jeans
FEET: No Slip Sneakers
HANDS: Unequipped
NECKLACE: Unequipped
EARRINGS: Unequipped
Ring 1:   Silver Claddagh
Ring 2:   Unequipped

ATTACK: 168
DEFENSE: 84
MAGIC ATTACK: 6
MAGIC DEFENSE: 12

PROFICIENCIES: Slapping Skill 49, Slapping Defense 10.1, Tree Climbing -5, Running 3.2, Tackling 1, Slashing defense 9.3, Light Armor 7.2, pizza cutter proficiency 12.3, pizza peel proficiency 7.2

Experience: 449/600

Upon seeing that he was level five, a smile spread across his face. He loved it when he could quantify his improvements. It's one of the things he loved about video games. This was a way to quantify improvements in real life. It was amazing. The jump in his attack surprised him. He still wasn't sure how attack and defense got figured.

The torn description to his shirt was concerning. Not only did it describe the shirt, but it also showed a minus one to the shirt's defense attribute. When comparing his slapping proficiency to his pizza cutter proficiency, Pete felt torn. He could keep leveling up his slapping, but he might fight monsters who are immune to slapping.

It was always good to stay balanced, relying on an arsenal of abilities in a fight. As such, he decided he'd need to hunt some of the tomato plants with a cutter. It would balance how he leveled his cutter and slapping skills.

He closed the prompt, kicked off his shoes, closed his eyes, and prepared to dose off. Then a loud crash sounded outside, jolting him up with a start.

18: I Think I'll Call You Pepperoni

Pete pulled his shoes on one at a time before pushing open his bedroom door and jogging through the bakery. A few paces past the tin door that went outside, he found Mod and Angel. He stopped next to them, observing the scared expressions on their faces.

The other citizens of the town shared Mod and Angel's fear. Most of those citizens stood by the open doors of their businesses and houses. They all looked in the direction of the town square. Pete cast his gaze in that direction, and his heart dropped.

It was the same giant turkey that had attacked him in the mountain forest. In a fit of rage, it knocked over carriages with its clawed feet. And it uprooted trees with its sharp beak, tossing them to the side without effort. Twenty feet from the monster, Nick the guard ran toward it, his sword drawn and ready to strike.

As the distance between them shrank, the notorious monster known as The Turkey Titan whipped its wing across Nick. The attack flung him into the air. Nick landed with a dull clank before he rolled to a stop. Undeterred, Nick began to rise again.

Pete considered the situation. Had the turkey followed him to town? Was this whole situation his fault? If it was, he had to do something. Even so, Pete was only level five. If Nick, a level ten guard, couldn't touch the creature, what chance did Pete have? After all, he was a pizzaman, a job that doesn't focus on combat. Pete took in a few deep breaths, gathering his courage. Then he charged toward the giant bird.

"Wait!" Mod and Angel both called out to him, but he ignored and pressed forward.

While he neared the creature, Pete lifted his

hand to slap and shouted the most appropriate battle cry he could come up with. "It's time for Thanksgiving!"

The turkey turned to Pete and swung its wing. The attack followed the same trajectory and speed as it had used on Nick.

Pete managed to dive under it: rolling to his feet, bending his knees, and jumping with as much strength as possible.

Pete's eyes widened with surprise as he pushed up into the air. He'd expected his strength bonuses from leveling up would help him elevate. Even so, he found himself thirty feet in the air, looking down at the turkey. With that kind of ups, he would have been the star player for any team in the NBA.

On his way down, he activated Steel Hands. When he reached the head level of the turkey, he slapped across its beak with a thwack. It squawked, stumbling to the side.

Pete's knees buckled as he landed, but he was able to keep his balance. When he looked at his enemy's health bar, he realized it had depleted by one-fourth. Corresponding prompts appeared:

The Turkey Titan attacked you. You Dodged!

You activated ability Steel Hands.

You attacked The Turkey Titan. You caused 140 damage.

You gained 10 jumping proficiency.

You gained 2.7 slapping proficiency.

You gained 6 evasion proficiency.

As the Turkey regained its balance, it shrieked

with rage and glared at Pete.

"Son," Nick the guard stepped next to Pete. "I appreciate the help, but you can't fight this. It goes outside the scope of your job."

"No, it doesn't," Pete explained. "I can turn that turkey into pepperoni, a meat topping for my pizzas."

Nick smiled, his bushy mustache accenting the smile. "Ah, I like how you think, son." Nick's name appeared with a corresponding health bar. It was straight below Pete's health bar on his battle menu, and a prompt appeared:

Nick Warman joins your party.

Where Nick liked how Pete thought, the turkey did not; it did not like anything about Pete. It charged at him, pecking its beak against the ground in a fast rhythm. Peck, peck, peck, peck, peck. Each peck brought it closer to Pete, spraying pebbles and dirt into the air, causing the ground to shake. And Pete ran in the opposite direction. He could hear the bird behind him; it was getting closer. Boom. Boom. Boom.

The beak lifted and dropped, this time pointed straight at Pete, the point ready to impale him. Pete dove to the side, avoiding the beak.

Though he avoided the sharp point, a shockwave caught Pete, lifting him and hurling him through the air. When he landed, it knocked the air from his lungs, and he let out an oof.

The Turkey Titan used machine gun beak. You received 27 damage.

The turkey remained so focused on Pete that it didn't notice Nick sneak behind it and attack it. In truth, Pete didn't notice him either, but he saw the prompt:

Nick the guard used Warrior's Sword. Critical Hit. Turkey Titan received 100 damage.

The message surprised Pete. His typical slap had caused more damage than a level ten guard's sword skill. Sure, Pete had boosted his attack with Steel Hands. Yet, he still expected Nick's sword to cause more damage than it had. Was Nick's sword that weak? Or was Pete's slapping overpowered? In the middle of the battle with the Turkey Titan, Pete didn't have time to contemplate it. When he returned to his feet, the turkey had refocused on Nick.

Pete looked at the distracted turkey. Its health bar was down to half its maximum. Two or three more hits and they could defeat it. Pete bent his knees and jumped at an angle.

The second his feet left the ground, he realized he put too much strength into his jump, and he slammed into the back of the Turkey Titan's head. It whined in surprise. Before Pete fell, he grabbed hold of feathers near its head and wrapped his legs around its neck. When he oriented himself, he realized he had mounted the turkey like a horse.

When he felt secure, he released his hand grip and began to slap back and forth. Slap, slap, slap. Without the Steel Hands effect active, the attacks didn't cause as much damage. Nonetheless, three of the weaker slaps was enough to deplete the turkey's HP in full.

"Wooooah!" Pete yelled as he and the turkey began to fall toward the ground. To prepare for the impending moment where they crashed, he hugged his arms around the monster's neck and braced.

A second later, they hit down, causing the earth to quake, shooting up a dust cloud beneath the mass of its vast body. Pete coughed and waved his hand back and forth in front of his face to push the dust away.

A coughing Nick the guard, walked through the cloud of dust, drawing near Pete. "That was great, son. Good job. I didn't realize you had it in you. Of course, I could have handled it by myself, but you made it easier. That is for certain."

Prompts appeared:

You defeated notorious monster The Turkey Titan.

Congratulations! You received 1000 experience points!

Nick Warman gained a level!

Congratulations! You gained two levels.

You received the following item drops: turkey bacon strips x 3,000, turkey pepperoni x 3,000, fingerless titan gloves, strong leather squares x 100, a titan's sword.

Before Pete had finished reading the prompts, Nick spoke. "I want all the bacon and the sword. Did you say the pepperoni is meat, too?"

Pete decided against answering Nick's question. He knew it would make negotiating for the items he wanted more difficult.

Pete already knew he wasn't getting any of the bacon.

He also knew he wanted all the pepperoni for the pizzeria. With half the leather, he'd have more than enough to craft high-quality uniforms for the pizzeria. The fingerless gloves looked cool and would give him some extra defense. "You can have all the bacon, half the leather, and the sword. I get the pepperoni, the other half of the leather, and the gloves. That is exactly half to each of us."

"Sounds fair," Nick stroked his chin before holding out his hand to shake Pete's. "You have yourself a deal."

As they shook hands, a new series of prompts came:

You received Turkey Pepperoni x 3,000

You received strong leather x 50

You received fingerless titan gloves

Pete put the gloves on, and another prompt appeared:

You learned Machine Gun Slap

Cool, Pete thought, happy to learn a new ability. After sorting the other items, Pete told Nick, "I expect you at the Mod's bakery tomorrow. I'll have a special surprise for you."

"An all meat pizza?" Nick asked.

Pete smiled. "That's possible, but I can't spoil the surprise. Make sure you stop by tomorrow, okay?"

"Son," Nick smiled ear to ear. "I'm sure it will be the highlight of my day."

19: Pizza and Games Part Two

Zoey loved bowling. It was one of her favorite things. It reminded her of all the summer nights spent at the bowling alley that her dad owned. She thought the sound she heard was bowling, but there was no crash of pins. Was it ski ball? It sounded too loud to be ski ball.

Come to think of it, she realized *everything sounds louder than usual*. The 80's video game music felt like it was blaring from speakers at a rock concert...

"Ugghhh," she groaned and forced her eyes open. Her head was lying on a table, and everything looked so fuzzy, out of focus. Did she forget to put her contacts in? Where was she? Through the fuzziness, she recognized a restaurant setting. There was a table across from her. A family ate at the table. On the other side of them, she saw the outline of what looked like arcade machines.

As she pushed herself into a sitting position, she heard a voice across from her. It was British and male from what she could tell. "Ah, good. You are awake. Usually, the process takes three days. I wasn't expecting you so soon. Pete will be happy to see you."

The usual process takes three days? Pete? What does any of this have to do with... When Zoey looked to the voice across the table, she stopped midsentence. "You're that cat in the tree, but you're a person... Are you a person? Everything looks super fuzzy right now."

"Ah, yes...it is fuzzy because of your contacts. You won't need them anymore." The cat said.

"This is one crazy dream." Zoey shook her head.

"It's not a dream." The cat assured. "My name is Max. Pete and I go way back. I thought he could use your help. Will you help him?"

"What's going on?" Zoey asked. "What you're saying doesn't make sense. Pete hates cats..."

"That's a hurtful thing to say."

"...and even if he didn't hate cats, talking cats aren't a thing. They don't exist."

"Talking humans don't exist," Max replied. "See. That doesn't feel good, does it? It hurts feelings. To be honest, I expected better from a friend of Pete."

"Okay, I'm sorry," Zoey didn't feel sorry, but she realized it was better to appease the cat and figure out what was going on. "Where am I?"

"Take out your contacts and see for yourself." The cat replied.

"Fine," Zoey thought the idea of taking out her contacts and seeing better didn't make any sense. Then she remembered how it worked for Spiderman. As she removed both lenses from her eyes, the world came to her in perfect clarity. She was in a Pizza and Games, and everything looked clear. It wasn't like 20/20 vision clear. It was like her eyes could zoom in and out. She could see across the room like she had a pair of binoculars.

Her sense of smell seemed sharper, too. The smell of pizza was overwhelming. Through that smell, she could smell the soda in the fountain machine.

"Do you see better now?" Max asked. She realized he was wearing a pink tank top with a lizard wearing sunglasses in its center. She looked at her own shirt. It was the same tank top. Max repeated. "I hope you see better now?"

"I can see." She answered, asking with an unusual calmness. "Why am I in a Pizza and Games? Why am I speaking with a cat at a Pizza and Games?"

"Would you prefer to be talking to their mascot mouse?" The cat slumped back, lifting his hand and wiggling a finger in the air. "I assure you that he is an excruciatingly boring mouse. He wears the hat to compensate. It's the same with the bear and the guitar. I am by far the most interesting animal here."

"You mentioned Pete," Zoey remembered. "What does Pete have to do with this?"

"You are familiar with isekai's, right?" Max inquired. When Zoey nodded yes, he continued. "I teleported Pete to another world to become its savior. After one day there, it became apparent to me that he would need some help. That's why you are here. Will you help Pete on his journey? Help might be too soft a word. Will you complete his quest for him? I am confident he can't do it alone."

"Pete is more capable than you think. He'll be able to do what needs done." She assured.

"He couldn't even close the prompt windows." Max held back a laugh. "It was great entertainment for sure, but not the trait of a world savior."

"Close the prompt window?" Zoey raised an eyebrow.

Max regained his composure. "Here is the deal. If you and Pete save the world known as Round, I will return you to your world known as Earth. I'll even return you to the time before I took you. Sound good?"

"Sounds like fun," Zoey said. "But before you send me there, how about some air hockey?"

"Air hockey?" Max wrinkled his furry cat forehead. "I'm sure that isn't necessary."

"Oh, and I'm sure it is," Zoey explained. "My dad always said never to do business with someone until after you've played them in air hockey. It can tell you a lot more about someone than you realize."

"That can't be true." Max glared. "Your dad did not do that."

"I assure you, Mr. Max. This is as true as the sky is blue. I mean during the day. It's been a long time since I've seen a blue sky. Ya know, 'cause I sleep during the day."

"Fine," Max Relented, swinging his legs out from the booth and standing. "When I win, you go to that other world, though."

Zoey laughed, standing and following Max through the restaurant. They passed children at play and arcade games until they came to the air hockey table. Zoey answered. "When I win, I go to that other world. No way will you beat me."

Max put two quarters into the machine, and it buzzed to life as the two took their places on each side of the machine. The puck came out on Zoey's side. She took it with her left hand, placing it on the table, using her other hand to take up her paddle. Then she fired a shot toward the goal where Max defended, ricocheting the shot off the right wall.

At that point, she realized something was wrong. The puck inched along at a painful, slow pace. It wasn't the usual power she put behind her signature shot. Instead, it reminded her of a four-year-old hitting the puck for the first time. How had she messed up to such an enormous degree?

The puck crawled along. One inch. Two inches. After what seemed like ten seconds, it reached Max's goal, and it slipped past him. Did he let it go in?

"Lucky shot." He glared. That response made it seem like he didn't let her score.

He took the puck and shot it toward her. The second he hit it, she began to focus, and the puck slowed again. Then she concentrated on the cat, and the cat slowed too. She watched as his eyes widened with excitement, a smile forming on his face. She hadn't hit the puck slow. Everything was moving in slow motion. Either that, or she was moving at a supernatural speed with inhuman reflexes.

When Zoey looked back down at the puck, it crawled in her direction. Instead of blocking it. She hammered her paddle atop the puck, pinning it to the table before aiming a straight shot at Max's goal. The puck flew past Max's paddle. "That's two goals to none." She told him, unsure of how she'd acquired her slow-motion skills. At the time, it didn't matter, though. What did matter was how she was winning.

Max growled and shot again.

This time, she waited until the puck was near and slammed it back in Max's direction. She scored again. "This is too easy." She laughed.

"Don't they teach sportsmanship on Earth? You could be a good winner." Max lectured.

"You're right." Zoey apologized. "I'm sorry. I mean, I've never played air hockey with such an awesome talking cat before." She added the last part because she decided it would be cool to have a talking cat as a friend.

Their game continued until Zoey reached seven points, making her the winner. More important to her, Max practiced impeccable sportsmanship the whole time. It taught her what she needed to know about the mysterious cat.

"Are you ready to go now?" Max asked.

"I am." Zoey smiled.

"Good," Max lifted his hand and snapped his fingers, creating a white light that engulfed Zoey.

Josh Walker

20: Raiders Part One

Cedric's job was thief, so he had to steal. The more things he could steal, the better he was at his job. But there weren't many opportunities to steal in Greenlake, not with Nick Warman doing his rounds.

As such, Cedric spent much of his time on the outskirts of town, in areas where the moderators' laws protected him from Greenlake's guard. When he was finding a mark, he preferred the mountain forest. It played to Cedric's strengths; he was small—a bipedal raccoon humanoid species no taller than three feet— with an uncanny propensity for stealth. At that size, within all the trees, it made it easy for Cedric to hide.

During the day, while patrolling his favorite thievery spot, Cedric followed sounds of combat and found a human. The man wore strange clothes, including a shirt with a hole in it and a funny hat. As Cedric observed, he watched the man move through the forest, fighting tomato plants.

So many things were strange about the circumstance. *I've never seen him in town*, Cedric thought; *I know everyone in town. Where did this man come from?* Cedric's initial impulse was to mug anyone weaker than him, and the man looked plenty vulnerable. Yet, Cedric knew looks could be deceiving. After all, he wore a worn leather cloak. It didn't seem like much, but it served its purpose. It kept him concealed from the world. Did the man's appearance serve a similar purpose? Did his appearance deceive?

Cedric didn't want to find out. Instead of mugging the man with a direct attack, Cedric decided to lure the Turkey Titan to do it. He kited it the whole way to the man, but the man got away. Cedric decided to learn more about the mark he missed, following the man to town.

There, he learned about pizza, stole, and ate two

of the delicious discs himself. He'd have saved some to share with the rest of his gang—the town called them the Trash Pandas—but the melted cheese and sweet tomato sauce tasted too good for him to resist.

Then the strangest thing happened. The man slapped the Turkey Titan, claiming whatever notable loot the turkey had to offer. It was loot that Cedric hoped to gain for his gang, but he knew he couldn't do it alone. He'd need help.

Cedric snuck his way back to the mountain, creeping with an absolute silence through the trees. Without making a sound, he climbed over and ducked under branches. Before long, he came to a mound covered by bushes and trees. The ridge was in an area near where the Turkey Titan used to inhabit. Cedric slid beyond the foliage and into a hidden cave entrance.

The cave widened to a diameter of five feet, burrowing into the mound twenty paces. From there, it branched into three tunnels.

During the early evening—early for a raccoon, anyway—sleeping raccoon humanoids covered the ground. Cedric took care not to step on them.

When he came to a fork in the tunnel system, he passed by some guards who were awake. They had the job of raiders, a vicious group of warriors who specialized in looting and combat. To match their job, they armed themselves with short swords, bows, and iron chain mail.

One hooted. "You better have brought home something worthwhile this time, or Rumpke is gon'a to be angry."

Another shouted. "Bladeater'll have your head this time if you don't bring him something good. Doesn't matter if you're his brother."

Rumpke the Bladeater was Cedric's older brother. In his childhood, Cedric received the job of thief. His brother received the appointment of warlord, inheriting their father's title. Title aside, the traits and skill trees for a warlord were so much better than a common thief.

If Cedric couldn't measure up, it wasn't his fault. He had more natural talent than his brother, but he didn't have the skill tree. If he was the one given warlord as a job, the Trash Pandas would run Greenlake. Even so, Cedric understood he was a common thief; he knew his place.

He continued deeper into the tunnel system, dim candles lighting his way. When he past by a table where four other raccoon humanoids ate scraps of rotten fruit and moldy bread, someone at the table taunted him. "Today'll be the day when your brother does you in. I hope you brought him something good this time."

Cedric ignored them, continuing toward his brother's chamber. It was a single room dug into the tunnel system at its far end. Two wooden doors provided the area privacy, a guard on each side, each armed with a rusty pike. As Cedric approached, the guard's snickered and pushed the doors open.

"Cedric," Rumpke's voice boomed as Cedric entered the room. Cedric looked to the stone throne where his brother sat. Rumpke wore a formfitting, steel harness. It showed off his six-pack and rippling biceps.

Bronze battle skirt covered him from his waist down to his knees. When standing, he was at least five feet tall, by far the largest of the raccoons. "Brother, it's good to see you today. Tell me. You do have good news, yes? You brought me something precious today? Something of value to our clan and kin?"

"Something precious, yes." Cedric watched a smile form on his brother's face. Cedric took it as a good sign, so he mustered a false bravado. "My dear brother, what I have for you is information."

Rumpke's smiled disappeared. "Not this again..."

"You don't need to worry," Cedric spoke quick. "This time, it is a sure thing. A man killed Turkey Titan. That monster had to have dropped a ton of loot. We can rob the man."

Rumpke the Bladeater scowled at his brother. "You don't see a problem with that?"

"A problem?" Cedric forced confusion into his voice. Though, he suspected what was coming next; he'd already prepared for it. He knew his brother well, knew what to say to manipulate him.

"You think it will be easy to enter into town and mug someone strong enough to fight The Turkey Titan?" Patience was leaving Rumpke's voice, annoyance replacing it.

"Nick Warman helped him beat the turkey," Cedric explained; his brother spat at hearing the name. "This single man by himself is only a level seven, someone named Pete. It was a strange name. I mean, I've never seen it before..."

"Get to the point," Rumpke growled.

"...right... The point is that this Pete stays at the bakery. He also hunts the tomato plants on the mountain. One way or another, we should be able to ambush him alone. At only level seven, I might be able to take him by myself, but I'd prefer one of your raiders to come with me. One of the level tens should do the trick. Give me one of them and three days. If you do that, I'll steal all his loot. Plus, I'll bring you a tasty treat called pizza. You'll love it."

"Three days?" Rumpke rubbed his forehead with two fingers. "All you need is three days?" He began to laugh. "And one of my level ten raiders?"

"It will be worth it." Cedric insisted.

"Do you even know what the loot was?" Rumpke asked, still laughing. "Sending out one of the raiders can draw a lot of attention. They stick out in a crowd, and Nick would be on them faster than your last girlfriend left you."

Cedric sighed. "Now, you are being hurtful. Brother, I'm asking you to trust me. I promise. I won't let you down."

"Fine," Rumpke said, cutting his laughter mid bellow and glaring at his brother. "But if you fail me this time, you don't get any more chances."

21: An Elf, a Mermaid, and a Cat

Pete woke early the next morning. When he stepped outside, the warm humidity hung in the air. He could almost feel it sticking to his skin. The temperature and cool breeze made for a comfortable ambiance. He inhaled a deep breath and continued through the town.

His first stop for the morning was at a wide building on the opposite end of the town. Above the front door, a sign hung. It read Timmy the Tailor.

Pete went through the front door. He froze in place, confused, a strong smell of leather filling his nostrils. To the left, he saw a rack set parallel to the wall. On it hung different designs and sizes of leather armor.

A glass display case was along the wall to the right. A careful shop owner had laid belts, wristbands, and other accessories beneath the glass. In a way, it resembled a game of Tetris, using every inch of space.

Someone had moved empty tanning racks to each of the back corners. Straps of leather hung from a wooden frame at the center of the racks. When in use, those straps would hold a hide in place for the sun to dry, turning it into leather. The frame attached to five-foot posts that formed legs on each side.

On the far wall, long rows of shelves held folded squares of leather and cloth. Two separate tables filled the room's center. One was a large square, one a long rectangle. The square table held what looked like tools for leatherwork. He wasn't familiar with any of them. The more extended table had spools of thread and needles.

At the leatherworking table, a woman sat. She was an elf with messy black hair that hung to her shoulders. She wore a blue leather tunic, black hose, and knee-high leather boots with buckles. A dusty apron covered her tunic; black, fingerless bracers protected her hands. She held an awl in her right hand.

Other tools were in a tool bag. A thick belt kept the bag on her left hip. As Pete entered the store, she stood and asked. "Can I help you, sir?"

"I'm...sorry..." Pete stuttered, thrown off guard by two things: the woman's beauty and the store's setup. "...umm... I hope I'm in the right place. That is to say... ummm... Is this the tailor? Timmy... was that his name? Was it something else? I'm not sure..." he gathered himself enough to finish his question. "Am I in the right place?"

"Timmy's my dad." She smiled. Laying the awl on the table. "My name is Tay. Can I help you with something?"

"Are you a leatherworker or a seamstress?" Pete asked.

"Yes," she answered.

"Which?" He let inquisitive wrinkles form on his brow.

She blinked, letting a neutral expression form on her face and tapping her chin. After three taps, she let a proud grin form on her face and answered with confidence. "Both. I can do both."

"Oh," Pete hesitated, gathering his thoughts, still distracted by the pretty seamstress... leatherworker... uh... both... "I guess that explains why I didn't see a leatherworker in town."

"That explains it." She agreed. "How can I help you?"

"Well, you see my shirt?" He asked. It was a dumb question. Of course, she saw his shirt. Unless she was blind... Was she blind? She didn't seem to be blind. "You aren't blind, are you?"

"Am I blind?" She laughed. "Of course, I'm not blind. What do you need? Wait. Let me guess. You need someone to repair the holes in your shirt?"

"How'd you guess?" He chuckled.

"I'm perceptive." She hopped up from the table

with an unnatural grace. It was almost like she floated back down to the ground, landing in a standing position. "Let me see." She glided over to him, placing her right palm near the hole on his shoulder. She ran the finger of her other hand along the torn cotton.

Pete tried to keep his cool. "So…ummm… You think you can fix it?"

"Yeah," she stepped back, placing a hand on each hip and tilting her head to the side. "Won't be too hard to fix. I can have it done in ten minutes."

"Great," Pete sighed with relief. "If it isn't too much trouble, I needed something else."

"Okay," she squinted her left eye and leaned forward, hands still on her hips. "I've heard this before. You aren't going to ask me on a date, are you?"

"What? No…of course, not…" He couldn't help but blush, eyes widening with embarrassment. He was quick to explain. "I needed pajamas and a swimsuit."

"Relax," she leaned back, offering a playful smile. "I was kidding. Pajamas, you said? I could make you a pair. What's a swimsuit?"

"It's like shorts but used for swimming. They go down past the knee." He used his finger to point to a spot on his shin. As the conversation became more familiar, he felt his blood pressure going down. "Like down to here."

"So, you need weird pants, pajamas, and repairs on your shirt?" She raised a questioning eyebrow. "But no date? You sure?"

"I'm sure…" He squeaked. As attractive as the elf was, Pete didn't know how long he'd be in Greenlake. He could save Round in a week and then be back on Earth. On the other hand, he could spend his whole life in Greenlake without ever fulfilling his role as Round's savior. Until things settled…until he knew what his new normal was…he didn't want to enter a relationship with anyone. Plus, he still liked Zoey. Even though they weren't a couple, going on a date with someone else would feel like cheating. He should have told Zoey how he felt while he still had a chance. "… How much will it cost?"

"No date, huh? Your loss." She shrugged, winking. "At least you know where I am if you change your mind."

Pete felt himself blushing again.

"As far as cost…" she pursed her lips to the side, pointing her eyes up, and then mumbling to herself before saying. "How does 60 len sound?"

"Sounds great." Pete agreed. "How long will it take?"

She pursed her lips to the other side. "Give me an hour."

"Cool…I'll see you then."

Fifteen minutes later, Pete found a quiet black sand beach along the lake. To ensure privacy, he'd picked a spot east of town. He'd never seen black sand before, so he examined it. Was it volcanic? It appeared to be. He thought it was cool. Aside from never seeing black sand, he'd never seen volcanic sand before.

Before jumping into the lake, Pete kicked off his shoes. When he went to empty his pockets, he remembered how all his items had moved to the void that was his inventory. He wasn't sure how it worked, but he figured they'd be safe there so long as he didn't summon anything while he swam.

With his pants still on—his shirt back with the seamstress named Tay—he inched his way into the shifting tide.

The wet sand tickled between his toes; the cool current lapped against his feet. The water was fresh and inviting. It reminded him of swimming in his neighborhood pool in the early fall. Even with the overcast sky, it was still warm enough to swim. Though, when winter came—he wondered if Greenlake had winters—he'd have to find a different way to take a bath.

With his first step, the water rose to his knee, sucking his jeans against his leg. He continued until he was waist-high. Then he dove at an angle, remaining below the surface and moving parallel with the coast.

As much as he enjoyed swimming on Earth, in Round, he felt like an Olympic gold medalist. He wasn't sure if it was his attribute bonuses from leveling up or his imagination. But for some reason, moving through the water seemed natural, effortless.

He could feel an undertow; it tugged at the whole of his body. Yet, it didn't scare him, and he pulled away from it, maneuvering with ease. He made a note of the potential hazard and decided to be safe and remain near shore.

Most days, he wouldn't waste so much time in the morning. But he hadn't bathed in so long, plus he had to wait for Tay to finish his commission, so he took advantage of the downtime. He zipped this way and that. He zoomed that way and this.

When he began to tire, he swam until he was knee-high and sat in the water. His legs declined down the eulittoral of volcanic sand. He let the tide rise to his chest before dipping to his waist. His only regret was that he didn't have any soap. He'd need to find some. If soap didn't exist, he'd need to figure out what the other people used.

He'd already learned they used a paste made from mint and clean leaves to brush their teeth. After, they'd rinse with an alcohol solution similar to Earth's mouthwash before spitting it out. He didn't know what clean leaves were, but with a happy heart, he had adopted the practice.

As he allowed his mind to daydream, he didn't notice the shadow beneath the surface, hidden on the other side of a dark, reflective water face. However, that shadow saw him, and it crept closer. In the mean-time, Pete closed his eyes, leaning back and taking in the sun as its rays began to pierce through the clouds overhead.

The shadow moved closer, unnoticed until feet separated it from him. It leaped from the water: splashing him in the face, sending adrenaline through his body, and causing him to jump back with a start. With frantic confusion, he kicked his legs and pushed himself backward with his arms like bicycle pedals. He didn't stop until he was out of the water.

When his eyes focused on his ambusher, he saw a girl's head staring back. She giggled, ducking back down beneath the surface.

He saw a scaley tail break the surface, propelling the girl back into the lake. Was she a mermaid? He guessed she was. He'd have to ask Mod about the lake later, see if it had mermaids.

As things were, it was time for him to retrieve his shirt, pajamas, and swimsuit. After, it was time for him to get to Mod's Bakery... No, he reminded himself it wasn't Mod's Bakery anymore... It was M and P's Pizzeria and Baked Goods. It was a long name. Pete decided he'd refer to it as the pizzeria for short. He sighed as he pushed himself to his feet and began back toward town.

Pete couldn't even see a seem where Tay had repaired the holes. With the repaired garb, he worked within the confines of the pizzeria. While Pete slapped out the dough and made the sauce, he found himself alone. Mod had gone to look for some cheese, sausage, bacon, vegetables, and other toppings for the pizzas.

If Mod couldn't collect all the ingredients Pete wanted, it wasn't the end of the world. It helped that Pete had the turkey pepperoni. Though, they knew the pepperoni wouldn't last forever, not even with three-thousand of them. To prepare for the future, Mod had brought some of the pepperonis to show them to the butcher. If the butcher could supply future pepperoni, they wouldn't have to worry about running out.

Pete hoped that Mod could gather a few other meats for the all meat pizza that Pete had promised Nick. In reality, he hoped Mod could gather all the meats so the pizza would have an appropriate name. Was it possible to gather all the meats? Pete knew it wasn't. Still, it wouldn't stop him from trying.

As Pete worked, he looked over the restaurant's new arrangement. They'd pushed some of the displays nearer the wall. That way, they could put two dine-in tables inside. They'd added two additional tables outside.

Later in the afternoon, the new pixie hires would show up for training. Everything seemed to be lining up. If they could make it through the next few days, the pizzeria would become famous. Pete refocused on the doughball in front of him, and he began to slap.

"You won't save the world by making pizzas all day." A voice spoke from one of the tables that had been empty.

This time, Pete didn't react. He was getting used to jump scares. Instead, he snapped his eyes toward the voice.

It was Max, sitting in one of the chairs. The cat's legs crossed under the table. He leaned forward with his elbows on the table, his fingers interlocked under his chin. Instead of a pink shirt, this time, he wore a white tuxedo with a black bowtie, a red cape draped around his shoulders.

"I won't be able to save the world." Pete snapped back. "If I don't know what I'm supposed to save it from. You left that part out."

"Oh," Max laughed. "So, I did."

Pete waited for Max to continue. When the cat

didn't, Pete prodded. "…and?"

"And I'm worried you need to figure out how to get stronger faster. You're taking too much time. You need to power level." Max told him.

Pete answered. "I can't PL. It's against the laws of the moderators. My alignment is lawful good. Literally, I can't break the law. It's on my character sheet."

"You can power level without breaking the laws of the moderators. You need to get creative." Max insisted. "Don't pretend you don't know how to follow the rules while still breaking the game. That's always how you played JRPGs on your home consoles."

Pete opened his mouth to protest, but what Max said was true.

Max continued. "You'd find a power leveling area and gain thirty levels, capping every skill and ability. Then you'd cruise to the end of the game, stronger than everything you came across. Right?"

"It's different here. I can't help you. You have the wrong guy." Pete hung his head. He loved the feeling of adventure he felt in Greenlake. Even so, if Round needed a hero, Pete didn't see himself as the best choice. It would be selfish for him to remain without fulfilling his role. "Can you send me back to Earth? Find someone else?"

Max lifted his palm to his face, scratching the top of his head with his fingertips and exhaling a breath of disappointment. "I'd expected better from you, Pete. I'll repeat it. You need to get creative. To help you foster your creativity…I've brought you…some help."

"Help?" Pete asked.

Instead of answering with words, Max lifted his hand and snapped. A familiar, blinding white filled the room. When it dissipated, Pete half-expected to find himself somewhere else. He didn't; he was still in the pizzeria.

When Pete looked around, Max was gone. Nonetheless, Pete noticed something else. Something that took his breath away. A woman was on the floor. She leaned back on her right elbow, shaking cobwebs from her mind, her left hand against her forehead. It was someone who Pete knew well; it was Zoey.

22: The New Employees

Pete hurried over to Zoey, kneeling next to her, using one of his hands to take her hand. He used his other hand to support her shoulder. "Zoey, are you okay?"

"Pete?" She blinked confusion from her eyes as he helped her to her feet, her eyes taking in the whole of the room. "Where are we?"

"It's hard to explain...harder to believe." Pete began. "I'll try to explain. There is this cat named Max—I'm not sure if he's good or bad—and he..."

"I know about Max." Zoey interrupted. Then she crossed her wrists before spreading her arms apart with her palms up. "I mean, where are we? What is this place?"

"Oh..." Pete's eyes widened. "Wait...you know about Max? How?"

"Well, he ran in front of my car one night, and I climbed the tree to save him." She sighed.

"And he jumped at your face, and you fell." Pete frowned. "It was the same trick he used on me."

"What?" Zoey began to giggle. "No, that's not it at all. I mean, he tried to make me fall, jumped at my face and everything. I kept my balance and got him down. You fell?" Her giggles became laughter.

"Yeah..." Pete snickered. "I guess I did. If you didn't fall, how did you get here?"

Zoey began to regain her composure. "I'm not sure. I remember handing the cat to the lady at the bottom of the tree. She seemed confused like she wasn't sure what to do next. It was like she wanted me to fall."

Zoey pursed her lips, stared into space, and shuddered before continuing. "Then that woman got this creepy smile. She had these sharp teeth..." Zoey refocused her eyes on Pete. "Next thing I knew, I was in a Pizza and Games talking to Max in human form.

After I beat him in air hockey, he sent me here."

"Air hockey?" Pete thought about what she had said. Zoey beat everyone in air hockey. She had the reflexes of… He stopped mid-thought, staring at Zoey with hopeful eyes. "Tell me you won."

Zoey nodded that she had.

Pete burst out laughing, crossing his arms over his stomach. Laughter continued to erupt; he couldn't help it. He stepped back, using one hand to support himself on the table, the other hand moving to his hip.

Zoey rolled her eyes at how ridiculous Pete looked. "I don't get it. What's so funny?"

"I'd say…you have the reflexes…of a cat." Pete choked out between the laughter, his face beginning to turn red. "But that doesn't work. You have…the reflexes…of a more than a cat…HA! HA! HA! HA!"

"It isn't that funny," Zoey flicked his hat off his head before smiling. "It's good to see you, Pete. When you didn't log on or come to work, you had me worried."

"Hey," he admonished, offering her a disapproving sneer. Then he bent over, picked up his hat, stood up, and repositioned it on his head, smiling and saying. "It's good to see you, too."

The pair stared at each other for a few more seconds, both incredulous of the situation in which they found themselves. Yet there they were, long time video game partners in crime, ready to experience a new world together.

But this time, it wasn't a video game. When they realized they were staring into each other's eyes, they both let shyness get the better of them and blushed. Then they hurried to avert their eyes.

To change the subject, Zoey moved to a bread display. She lifted a roll, tossing it in the air and asking. "So…why do you have a name and level seven above your head? Also, let's get back to my first question.

Where is this place?"

With a clearer head than before, she took in the room for a second time. Her eyes stopped on the doughballs and slapped crusts on the counter. Her eyes darted back to Pete. "Tell me you didn't."

"I did. I turned the town's bakery into a pizza joint." He lifted his eyes back to her and shrugged. "I like pizza and this world—the world is called Round, by the way—it didn't have pizza. Someone had to make it. Not to mention, my job on my status screen is piz-zaman. "All the quests I get center around making piz-za and helping the owner of this bakery. In the process of doing quests, we've turned his bakery into a pizzeria slash bakery thingy. As far as my name and level go... When you focus on someone or something—like the tomato plant monsters outside of town—their name and level appears above their head. I've noticed the colors change so that you can always read them against the background. It's cool."

Zoey's eyes widened with excitement. "Say that again."

Confused, Pete repeated. "I invented pizza here and established the first pizzeria?"

Her excited expression became a glare. "The other part."

"I like pizza?" He guessed.

"The other part." The intensity of her scowl in-creased, annoyance filling her voice.

"Names and levels? Colors change?"

"No," She growled.

"Status screen?"

"YES!" Her voice cracked as she bounded over to Pete. Max had mentioned closing prompts before. Zoey had come to understand what the cat meant. "That. You have a job? You have status screens? When are we going to go leveling? Can we form a party? Do you have spells and magic? Do I have magic? What's my job? Tell me how to use everything. I need to know. This is," she inhaled a deep breath and let it out as she said the last word, "aawwweesooomme."

"I was about to apologize for getting you involved in all this," Pete told her. "Does this mean I don't have to apologize?"

She held up the pointer finger of her right hand. "One, this wasn't your fault. Max did it to us." She held up a second finger. "Two, this is the coolest thing ever. Instead of watching isekai, we are isekai." She held up a third finger. "Three, you better answer my question. How do I get to my status screen? Don't make me flick your hat off again."

"You think about it," Pete explained. "When you will it to be, it appears in front of your face."

"That's it?" She leaned toward him. "You sure there isn't anything else to it?"

"One hundred percent sure, Zoey." He confirmed. "Try it."

"Okay," she moved her head to each side to stretch her neck. Then rolled her shoulders. Then she moved her arms back and forth in unison. It was like she was getting ready for a P.E. class. "Here goes. Status screen, appear!" She held out her hand as if summoning a spell from her fingertips. Then she lurched her head back like it was about to slam into something. "Whoa! There it is. This is so cool."

Before she had a chance to look at all of it, the door to the restaurant opened. Mod moved into the doorway and stopped, his eyes fixating on Zoey. "Pete, did you know there is a person in here with you?"

"I did know that," Pete answered as Zoey turned her eyes to the side so she could see Mod around the prompt blocking her vision. She couldn't figure out how to close it. "This is Zoey. She's one of my friends, and she makes a better pizza than I do. When the pixies start this afternoon, she'll be a great help with teaching them. That is. If she's up for it?"

"I'm up for it." She gave a thumbs up.

Pete directed his next sentence at Zoey. "This is Mod. He owns this bakery."

Still looking at Mod with her eyes pointed to the side, she told him. "It's nice to meet you."

"It's nice to meet you, too," Mod responded. When he saw how she looked at him, he wrinkled his forehead. "Are you okay? Is something the matter?"

Pete realized what was going on and stifled a giggle.

"Nothing's the matter," Zoey answered. "I'm stretching my neck. It's a little stiff from my journey here."

"Journey?" Mod began toward an empty space on the counter and began to materialize cheese, vegetables, and meats over its surface. "Cool. You must have come a long way. Where do you hail from?"

"Cheyenne," She replied, "Same as Pete."

While Mod's back was to them, Pete leaned his mouth to Zoey's ear, whispering in her ear how to close the prompt. She did as told, and the prompt dissolved out of existence.

"Pete never told me where he was from," Mod explained, looking back at her as he continued materializing toppings. "What is Cheyenne like?"

"Some people like it." She looked straight at Mod this time. "Some people think it's boring. It's like anywhere...I guess. It has its positives and its negatives. It's all about what a person wants. Ya know?"

A smile crept across Mod's face. "That is so true. Sometimes I think about leaving here, but everything I know is here. I love it most days and long for something greater other days. I understand exactly what you are saying."

As Mod and Zoey continued to speak, Pete moved over to look at the toppings on the counter. The meats included sausage, ground beef, Canadian bacon, real bacon, and thin slices of steak. With the turkey pepperoni they already had, Nick was getting his all meat pizza. *I hope you like it, old man.*

Angel zipped through the open window, followed by the triplets, followed by four other pixies whom Pete hadn't met. With military precision, they formed a line facing mod, hovering at face level and saluting. As Mod, Zoey, and Pete looked at the pixies, Angel said. "The new recruits are here and ready to work, Mod. Tell us what to do."

"I'll defer to Pete and his friend Zoey," Mod nodded toward Zoey. "They are the pizza experts. I'm still learning myself."

"Zoey," Angel turned toward Zoey. "Nice to meet you. I'm Angel."

"Nice to meet you." Zoey smiled. "I always wanted to meet a pixie."

"You've never met a pixie before?" Angel's jaw dropped; the respective jaws of the other pixies dropped, too.

Zoey forced a soft reverence into her voice. "Nope, I come from a place where only humans live. Meeting amazing people like you and your friends is one of the reasons I'm glad I came here."

Angel smiled. "Swag. I'm glad you're here. Let me introduce you to the others. The triplets are Skye, Hope, and Tornado." Angel pointed to each in order. When she said Tornado, Tornado spun in a circle, repeating his name. "This is Rice and Tice." Angel nodded at the two tallest pixies. "They're brothers." Angel moved her eyes to the next pixie over, a girl with dark hairs and black wings. "This is Shy. She wants to be an actress someday."

"Cool," Zoey said, "me too; that's awesome."

True to her name, Shy broke eye contact, looking at the ground and leaning her upper body away.

"Cool."

Angel pointed at the last pixie. "This is Nolan…"

"That's not my name." Nolan continued to stare straight ahead with his green eyes. He had a stern expression on his face, bangs from his full red hair hanging in front of his eyes.

"Right, right, right," Angel said. "I forgot. He wants you to call him Guitar-man."

"That's right," Nolan confirmed, keeping the stern expression while lifting his arms to play an air guitar. After three seconds, he snapped his arms back to his side."

"It's nice to meet each of you," Mod told them. "I look forward to us working together."

"They look forward to working for you, too," Angel spoke for them. "Right, guys? From stonks to riches right here."

Pete, Zoey, and Mod didn't know what stonks were, but they appreciated the sentiment.

The pixie's responses came in unison: Nolan air guitared, Tornado jumped and spun, Hope danced. She swung her arms from front to back while twisting the ball of her foot on the floor. It was like combining the floss with the mashed potato. Skye dabbed to one side then the other. Shy blushed. Tice and Rice high fived.

"Awesome," Zoey told them. "Let's learn how to run a pizza restaurant."

Zoey and Pete moved to the counter and began to show the pixies how to prep each topping. At Pizza Place, they kept toppings in tubs. At Mod's, they could keep the toppings in each of their individual inventories.

They didn't worry about teaching the pixies how to slap the dough or saucing a pizza because the pixies weren't big enough to do those things. Instead, they trained the pixies in customer service. The pixies learned how to greet, take an order, and assign an order for delivery.

"Tonight," Pete explained, "Tell all the customers about how we will offer delivery. If they ask what delivery is, tell them it means they can call any of your communication boxes during our pizza hours. Those hours are from three to seven at night. Tell them that they can order food that way, and we will bring it to their house."

"I have a question." The pixie named Nolan raised his hand. "Why aren't we open longer or at lunchtime?"

"At the moment," Pete told him, "We haven't figured everything out yet. When we get more comfortable, we will start to do more hours."

"Any other questions?" Zoey asked.

No one had any.

"Good," Mod said. "Thank you for your hard work. I have one more rule before we start..." he looked at Pete, "what was the phrase, again?"

"Slinging pies," Pete replied.

Mod nodded, "One more rule before we start slinging pies." The pixies remained attentive; their eyes fixed on him. "That rule is to have fun. I want this to be the best place to work in Greenlake."

"Swag," all the pixies said in unison, and the afternoon's work began in earnest as the customers started to pour in. Some of the customers were returning; some were new.

Pete didn't think the pixies were big enough to slap dough. He hadn't realized their creativity would allow them a way to learn on their own. He discovered this when the pixies sent Shy up to him during the last three minutes before the store closed. The others stood behind her with hopeful faces.

She held out a pixie sized pizza, holding it out for Pete.

"That is adorable," Zoey said. "I didn't know pizza could be cute… But that is one cute pizza."

"Do you want me to bake it?" Pete asked.

Shy nodded while keeping her eyes adverted downward.

"We can do that," Mod told her. "Did you have any other questions; did you need anything else?"

Shy shook her head no, turning to flutter back to the other pixies who spun, air guitared, and high-fived each other.

As they celebrated, a customer pushed through the door. He was a type of raccoon humanoid, a species Pete hadn't come across, no taller than three feet. The customer wore a brown leather cloak, stereotypical of thieves in roleplaying games. On instinct—as a pizzaman—Pete distrusted raccoons, but he tried to work past his instincts. To do this, Pete stepped up to the counter. "Welcome to M and P's. How can…"

The raccoon brandished a dagger. "I want everything that dropped from Turkey Titan, and every len you earned tonight. If you give me that, no one gets hurt."

Pete realized he should have trusted his instincts. Nonetheless, a raccoon had already stolen from him once in his life. He wasn't going to let it happen again. He activated slap'm silly, lifted his hand, and swung it across the would-be thief's face.

The raccoon creature fell in a slump.

Josh Walker

23: Raiders Part Two

From his hiding spot, the raider named Ragoon watched as Pete slapped Cedric. When it happened, Ragoon gasped in horror. Had that man killed Cedric with one slap? At only level seven? That seemed impossible.

How was Rumpke going to take it when he found out his brother was dead? Sure, all the Trash Pandas like to tease Cedric, and Rumpke would threaten his brother from time to time. But that didn't mean Rumpke wanted his brother dead. Would Rumpke blame Ragoon for it? If so, Ragoon was as good as dead, too.

Ragoon caught his breath when he realized Cedric wasn't dead, only unconscious. In fact, Cedric still had all his HP. After that, how did he have all his HP?

Ragoon looked at the others in the room. One of the pixies was on their communication box, no doubt calling the local guard, Nick Warman.

It didn't give Ragoon any time to plan or organize Cedric's rescue. The best Ragoon could do was go back to the hideout and let Rumpke know what happened. Should he go back? No, Rumpke might still blame him for Cedric's capture. He'd punished others of the Trash Pandas for less. Then again, did Ragoon have any other options?

He always wanted to go to the capital and get a legitimate job in waste management disposal.

He sighed, knowing he didn't have enough len saved up to leave Greenlake. Besides, Rumpke would know how to save his brother. Ragoon wouldn't get in trouble. Or would he? He reconsidered a rescue attempt. He could try to save Cedric. How much time did he have before Nick arrived? Could Ragoon defeat Pete? Could he handle the two humans, the elf, and the pixies at the same time? He focused on the human girl.

She was only level one. It would make her an easy target. Ragoon felt disgusted by how someone could reach adulthood without gaining any levels. He'd seen it happen before, but he didn't understand it.

He turned his eyes to the baker, a level seven elf. Even though he wasn't familiar with a baker's skill tree, Ragoon was sure he could take a level seven.

He considered the pixies. Adult pixies had a unique talent to manipulate the wind and elements. These pixies seemed too young for that. The most potent spell they'd know would summon a dust devil at most.

That left the blond-haired, blue-eyed human...

After careful but hurried consideration, Ragoon decided to abandon Cedric. On his way out of town, he remained in the alleys. On the outskirts of town, he stuck to the grass and crops in the fields.

A short time later, he made it to the mountain and the treeline. Therewithin, he found privacy from any who might have seen him. As he climbed the hill, he kept his pace slow, not anxious to return to Rumpkin.

The cool night air whistled and rustled the branches around him. It also reminded him they were entering fall. It was one of his favorite seasons. And it held Harvestfest, his favorite holiday. Ragoon had a great costume picked out for the occasion. He'd wear it to the party that the Trash Pandas always put on during the holiday.

What was he doing thinking about holidays? First, he had to survive his upcoming interaction with Rumpke. He chided himself and hurried the rest of the way to the entrance of the Trash Panda's lair. When he arrived, he shoved through the foliage covering the cave opening.

At that time of night, the cave was almost empty. The rest of the gang had gone to rob, steal, loot, and scavenge for all the loot and food they could get their hands on. Only a few guards and raiders remained. They spaced themselves at even intervals throughout the tunnels. They saluted Ragoon as he passed by them.

When he reached Rumpke's chamber, the guard stationed on each side of the door pushed it open. Ragoon stepped through the open doors. A few steps in, and the doors closed behind him.

Rumpke sat in a corner, a pile of knives, short swords, and ninja stars on the table in front of him. Rumpke shifted the weapons around, organizing them. Without looking up from the weapons, Rumpke asked, "how did it go? I know Cedric can be difficult to work with, but he means well."

As Rumpke had begun to speak, Ragoon stopped, standing at alert. When Ragoon started to talk, he saluted, hitting the palm of a closed right fist against his left shoulder. Then he held it there. "Sir, they captured Cedric."

Rumpke stopped sorting the weapons, looked up at Cedric, and frowned. "And you somehow got away?"

"Only to inform you, my lord." Ragoon struggled to keep his composure. "As it turns out, the human who killed the Turkey Titan is powerful. I would not have been able to face him my..."

"Did I not send you, Ragoon," the fur on every inch of Rumpke's muscular form stood on end, and his scowl intensified, "to protect my brother?"

"You did, sir," Ragoon replied. "But, I thought..."

"I don't pay you to think." Rumpke roared, standing and knocking over his chair. Then with slow, precise movements, he lifted his arms to each side. His arms bent at the elbow, clawed pointer finger touching clawed thumb on each hand. He lowered his hands that way, expelling a slow breath and saying, "okay... okay... We've got this. We can fix this. Mom would want you to fix this. You need to save your brother."

"Sir?" Ragoon remained saluting. "We can save your brother with a trade."

Rumpke let his hands fall to his side." A trade? What kind of trade?"

"Pete, the one who killed the Turkey Titan and captured your brother," Ragoon explained. "He has a friend, a level one human woman."

"Level one?" Rumpke spat. "How disgusting and weak."

"Yes," Ragoon agreed. "We can capture her and use her in a trade for your brother's safe return."

"Let's go with your plan, Ragoon," Rumpke told him. "Gather the rest of the raiders together. We need to be careful this time. We need to plan. This Pete is becoming more trouble than is good for him."

24: Uniforms

Hope, Skye, and Tornado returned home that night, bringing a pixie sized pizza with them for their mom and dad to try. It was already late, so they went to bed.

Yet, Hope didn't sleep. She tried to, but she was too excited to sleep. Designs for the pizzeria uniforms danced through her mind; her creativity itched to get out. Before she blinked, her hands needed to draw what was in her mind's eye.

Good thing she kept a sketchpad next to her bed. She reached over and snatched it. Then she grabbed the box of oil pastels that she kept under her pillow, and she began to work.

She began with the logo, designing one that was a traditional, white Chef's hat. On the cap, the initials M&P rested above the image of a pizza. One slice of the pizza was away from the others. Though, its point still occupied the space that its absence created in the pizza.

Next, Hope started on the pixie uniforms. The female uniforms used over-the-knee stockings with combat boots. A black, pleated skirt covered a puffy underskirt. A white, halter neck, button-down shirt tucked in at the waist.

A dark blue corset went over the halter neck. It had vertical, black stripes running up and down on each side.

A wide belt wrapped over the corset. The belt was brown with two large grommets near the top and bottom on each side. From the top holes, a chain ran across the front of the uniform, hanging at a slight arc. The bottom grommets connected with a parallel chain.

Sleeves with the pizzeria logo covered the forearms. The cherry on top of the uniform was the little, black bowties.

The male pixies' uniforms used the same belts and combat boots. But for their tops, they used long-sleeved, button-up white shirts. The sleeves ended in wide cuffs.

Dark blue, padded vests were over the shirts. The vests had stripes running up and down like on the girls' corsets. The bar on the right side had buckles to put on and take off the vest. A brown pad with vertical stripes covered each shoulder.

On their left shoulder, they wore a patch with the store logo. For pants, they wore simple black trousers.

Next, she made Mod's. His would be a human-sized version of the ones the male pixies would wear.

For Pete, she knew he needed something that would withstand combat. She saw what the tomato monsters had done to his shirt before. Even so, it still needed to match the other uniforms.

She began with black, leather pants tucked into dark blue, leather combat boots. To protect Pete's upper body, he'd wear a padded white shirt with long sleeves. Over the shirt, he'd have a dark blue leather vest. A black bandoleer ran from his left shoulder to his right hip.

The last person to need a uniform was Zoey. Hope wasn't sure if Zoey would fight monsters with Pete or stay in the store. As such, Hope wasn't sure if to make it from cloth or something more durable. She decided to err on the side of caution, and she began to draw.

A dark blue leather corset covered a black, padded vest. Unlike the corsets on the pixie uniforms, Zoey's was a form of legitimate armor, thick and durable. It would protect her against slashing attacks. Black, leather bracers protected her forearms, both bracers boasting the pizzeria's logo.

A steel skirt hung over black shorts. Over-knee-stockings combined with leather padding at the knee.

She'd have the same combat boots as the other uniforms.

All the uniforms had hats. Mod's would be the same baker's hat as always. The only difference would be the company logo front and center.

Everyone else would have a hat like pizzas with the bill. Pete had called it a baseball cap. Hope didn't know what baseball was, but she knew how to draw the hats. All of them had the same company logo. Pete's and Zoey's would be made of sturdy leather instead of fabric.

By the time she finished her designs, it was three in the morning. With her work done, she closed her eyes, and in an instant, she was asleep.

As the sun rose, she awoke with a renewed vigor. For only four hours of sleep, it didn't seem normal to be so full of life. But the excitement she felt for her designs energized her. She couldn't wait to share them.

At the breakfast table, she finished fast, asked permission from her parents to go out, and hurried to the pizza restaurant: knocking on its tin door, hoping someone would be there, her elation building.

*   *   *

Ting. Ting. Ting. Mod recognized the sound. It was the door to his restaurant. "Coming," he shouted as he pulled a pie from the oven. He set it on the counter before hurrying to the front door.

He wasn't used to guests that early in the morning, so he wondered who it was. When he reached the door, he wiped his eyes with his forearm to clear flour from them. Then he pulled open the door.

"I finished the job you gave me." Hope zipped in before Mod could greet her. "Look at these. I have costumes for everyone." She began to lay her designs over a table, talking fast without taking a breath. "The pixies have their own uniforms, Pete has one, Zoey has one, and I made one for you, Mod. Look. There is a logo, too. We should get a sign." Hope's eyes widened. "Do you think I can design the sign?"

Mod smiled. "Let's look at these designs first, and we'll go from there." He picked up one of the sheets and began to look it over. "These look amazing, Hope. You did a great job. I love the logo. It's my hat with a pizza on it." He grinned. "We can't afford a sign yet. But when we can, you have the job of designing it."

"Thank you." Hope smiled ear to ear. "I worked hard on these. They were a lot of work."

"This morning, Pete was going to show Zoey the town. While they are out, I'll have them stop by the smith and the tailor so they can commission your designs with Joey and Tay."

"I hope they make them fast." The small pixie hugged her hands to her chest. "I'm so excited."

25: Can Vampires Eat Pizza?

When Pete woke up, he was on a pile of hay in the corner of the room where Mod let him stay. He looked to where Zoey slept in the bed. She lied above the blanket, arms crossed over her chest. She looked so peaceful, he decided to let her sleep.

With haste, he changed from his pajamas to his Pizza Place clothes and snuck into the bakery's sales area. Once there, he noticed Mod speaking with Hope near one of the dine-in tables. "Hi, Hope. You're here early today." Pete told the pixie.

"Hurry, over here, Pete." Hope waved with her right hand, pointing down at the table with her left. "You have to see our uniforms."

Pete hurried over as commanded and looked at the drawings. "These are amazing. You did this yourself?"

"Yessir," she landed on the table and began to do her version of the mashed potato next to the drawings. "I stayed up super late. Like it was super late. It was so late. Then I did them all. Then when I finished, I went to bed. It was hard work."

Mod entered the conversation. "Pete, I'd like you to take those to Tay and Joey. Commission them to make their respective parts of the uniforms.

Pete blushed when remembering his encounter with Tay from the previous day.

"Is something wrong?" Mod asked.

"No, nothing." Pete fibbed. "Everything is good. I'll take Zoey, and we'll take care of this. No problem. If their past work is any indicator, we will have new uniforms today."

"Pete," Zoey's voice came from a crack in the bedroom door. "I need some help."

"Right," Pete shouted back, looking in the direction of the bedroom. It surprised him that Zoey was awake; she appeared to be in such a deep sleep before. "I'll be right there." Pete turned back to the pixie. "And you keep up the good work. I love your creativity."

Pete padded back to the room and looked at the door. It was still cracked open. He held the doorknob and knocked. "Can I come in?"

"Yes…" Her answer seemed meek, not characteristic of Zoey.

Pete pushed the door open, finding Zoey sitting on the edge of the bed, staring gat him with wide eyes.

"What's the matter?" Pete asked, sitting next to her.

"Last night, I didn't get a good chance to look at my status screen." She began, a somber tone in her voice. "I was going to look at it. Then Mod came in, and I was so focused on closing the prompt that I forgot to read it. This morning, I looked at it…and…I have some questions…" She looked down. "And some concerns…"

"What questions and concerns?" Pete put his hand on her shoulder. "What's wrong?"

"Pete," She turned her eyes to him. "On your status screen…the part that says race…what does it say for your race?"

"Human…why?"

"On mine," she explained. "It says I'm a vampire…"

"A vampire?" Pete smiled. "You're joking, right? Pulling my leg?" When she shook her head no and smiled, showing her long fangs. "Oh, man." Pete drew back. "You are a vampire."

"I am a vampire," she nodded.

"Do you want to…you know…eat people?" Pete asked.

"I was fine eating the pizza." She told him. "It filled me up, gave me energy, and everything. I mean, since I don't know what blood tastes like, it's hard for me to crave it, right?"

"I guess," Pete agreed, stroking his chin between his thumb and finger. "We will have to ask around, find out what we can about vampires. Until we know more, we shouldn't tell anyone about you being one."

Mod's voice called from the dining area. "You guys okay in there?"

"We're fine. We'll be right out," Pete shouted back. Then he turned to Zoey, asking. "You ready for the day? Wait…does sunlight hurt you?"

"I'm not sure," She admitted.

"Well, let's find out," Pete said, standing and moving to the window with closed curtains. He lifted his hand and grabbed the inside of the curtain. "Ready?"

She moved to a corner away from the window and nodded.

He cracked open the curtain, letting a sliver of sunlight beam in.

"It gives me a headache." She explained. "I don't like it, but I'm not afraid of it or anything." She moved closer to it, creeping within inches of where the beam created a small rectangle on the floor. Then she touched it.

Nothing happened. The direct light didn't burn her. It didn't hurt. It warmed her hand like usual. Looking at it gave her a headache, though. She looked at Pete and explained. "I need a cloak, or sunglasses, or something. The light doesn't hurt me. Even so, going out in the sun without something to keep it from my eyes sounds excruciating."

As luck had it, Mod kept a hooded cloak in his store. When they asked to borrow it, he seemed confused. Why would someone need a heavy cloak in the warmer, fall weather? Even so, he relented, lending it to Zoey.

After this, Zoey and Pete began toward the smith with Hope's designs, ready to commission the new uniforms.

As they walked, Pete explained the basics of how to open and close an inventory. Then he asked, "Do you have a job? A job tree?"

From beneath the cloak, she smiled. "yes. I have one."

"Well," Pete asked. "What is it?"

"Same as always." She said.

"No way..." Pete grinned. "You are a vampire Paladin? Is that allowed?"

"I guess." She shrugged.

"Have you looked at the job tree yet?" He asked.

"I have a job tree? That's awesome." She questioned. "How do I open it?"

Pete explained, "You think about it, and it pops up."

"There it is," she confirmed. "How do I get job points?"

"You need to do job-related quests," Pete explained. "I'm not sure how to get them. Mine popped up on their own as I started making pizza." Pete pulled up his own job screen, showing he had more job points than he had before. It must have been from leveling up after he defeated the Turkey Titan. "It looks like I've received them every time I level up, too." He closed it.

"How did you get experience to level up?" She asked.

"For me, it came from beating these tomato plant monsters. It was like the points tied to the quest I got. I'm still trying to figure it out for sure." Pete explained. "That reminds me. I guess they have a law here that you can only level up by doing things related to your job."

"What do you mean?" Zoey questioned. "Like no power leveling?"

"Exactly," Pete scratched under his right eye with his right finger. "They call it a law of the moderators. It seems the moderators don't like people getting too much stronger than other people."

"That's lame." Zoey sighed.

At that point, they reached the smith.

When they arrived, the smith worked outside at the anvil. He was in the middle of his typical heating, cooling, and pounding metal routine. When they neared him, he didn't look up. He used his tongues to hold up a piece of metal and said. "Hey, guys…look at this."

It was a round cylinder that tapered on each end. A three-inch diameter reminded Pete of a tail-pipe's muffler. "Nice," Pete said. "What's it for?"

"Dude, it'll be awesome. You don't even know." Joey the smith grinned. "But I'll have to show you when I finish. I don't want to ruin the surprise."

"I look forward to it," Pete said. "We have another commission for you.

"Sounds like fun." He grinned. "What did you have in mind this time?"

"Have you been to Mod's bakery in the last two days?" Pete asked.

"Dude," the smith smiled. "The pizza is so good. Not as good as some of Wanda's weird drinks for boosting energy, but pizza is close."

Zoey giggled and whispered so only Pete could hear. "It's like all the caffeine drinkers back in the store. They love their energy drinks."

Pete smiled in agreement.

The smith continued. "You need something for the store? For the pizzas?"

"Actually," Pete materialized Hope's designs. "I have these images for you. Let me show them to you."

The smith looked at the drawings. At the same time, Pete explained which parts would be metal, their sizes, and how many he would need. "Do you think you can do it?"

"No problem." The smith grinned. "I can have all

this done in an hour. Come back then."

"Will do," Pete said. "Wait...how much will it cost?"

"200 len." Mod had given Pete len to cover the charge. Even so, 200 len was a big hit. Then again, they needed uniforms.

"Alright," Pete smiled. "We'll be back in an hour."

As they walked away, Pete looked at Zoey. "It's time to go to Wanda's."

"Wanda's?" Zoey asked. "Why?

"Two reasons," Pete explained. "One, I've never been there, and I'm dying to see what's inside. Two, you said you needed sunglasses. If anywhere in Green-lake is going to have them, it will be Wanda."

26: Wanda's Weird Windmill (of Wonderous Widgets and Wild Waffler)

When Pete and Zoey entered Wanda's, they didn't know what to expect. What they found was a dark sales floor. There were no neat rows, no tidy walk spaces.

Instead, the aisles zigzagged around shelving. Most of the shelves had two to three shelves. But some of the shelves went twelve rows up and touched the ceiling. Other shelves hung from the ceiling, dangling at eye level in the middle of an aisle. Pete and Zoey had to duck to get under those.

Items for sale included radiant neon liquids in glass bottles, bright crystals, and shimmering bits of ore. Glowing posters covered the walls and ceiling. Trinkets hung all over the room, spinning on invisible strings. They refracted or radiated shifting beams of light.

As Pete and Zoey browsed—neither of them sure what anything was—they reached the back wall. A single propeller adjoined to the center of the wall. It spun, so its blades missed the ceiling, floor, and walls by inches. The weird thing was how the back wall was a rectangle, wider than it was tall. Even so, the propeller shrank and extended to match its space.

"I guess that's why they call it a windmil ," Zoey said.

"I guess so," Pete agreed.

"It is. Indeed, it is. Much a lot, indeed it is." an old lady appeared behind them. The voice sounded old and feminine, with a hint of mischievous kindness. "People always said it never made sense to out the propeller on the inside of a windmill. I showed them. Then they saw it. Some understood. Some didn't. I'm glad you did."

Pete looked at the woman. She was short and plump with long, messy hair. The hair was jet black with streaks of white. She wore a pointed, purple witch's hat with yellow stars and red and orange planets all over it. Thick, black goggles covered her eyes.

She wore a purple jacket over a yellow vest over a white collared shirt. They folded, blended, and tucked into each other. The only place where Pete could tell where one began and the others ended was at the collar. There, three rows worth of collar stuck up around her neck.

A puffy purple skirt was high on her waist. A second leather skirt hid underneath it, going down to her knees. Striped black and white tights hid beneath the skirt. Black curled toe shoes seemed to tap as the woman stepped closer, asking. "Welcome to Wanda's. Can I help you today?"

"Yeah," Zoey began. "I'm look…"

"You're a vampire." Wanda interrupted, tapping as she stepped closer. "Oh, how exciting. I've never had a vampire in my store before. What an exciting day. Is it day? Is it night? Should I get a watch or a clock? Do you have a clock?"

"Umm…at home, I have a few," Zoey answered. "In Greenlake, the only one I have is on my communication box." Zoey materialized her cellphone to show it.

"Oh, that's very nice." Wanda nodded. "I know what you're going to ask next. How does Wanda get wind to make the windmill's propeller spin? It's a simple answer. I'm a witch. I have magic. I magic the wind. Poof. Problem solved. Magic wind equals an indoor windmill. I do what I want."

"Right," Zoey smiled. "It's all about girl power."

"Exactly," Wanda looked at Pete while pointing at Zoey. "Your girlfriend is a smart one."

"What!?" Pete and Zoey said together, Pete adding. "She's not my girlfriend."

At the same time, Zoey clarified. "He's not my boyfriend."

"Oh," Wanda blinked, confused. "But you will be together like that at some point. I don't mean to get ahead of myself, but if you aren't ahead, you're behind. That's why I get ahead of myself with this topic."

Pete and Zoey blushed.

"So how can I help you?" Wanda pulled down her goggles, letting them hang around her neck. "Did you need something special?"

"Actually," Zoey said. "I was hoping for something to protect my eyes in the sun. Do you have sunglasses? Do sunglasses exist in Round?"

"Sunglasses?" Wanda considered the word. That's a fantastic word. "Glasses, but you wear them in the sun...I don't have any of those here, but I have something that might help you. Please, follow me."

They walked with her, rounding one of the shelves. "I haven't seen you two before. Are you new to Greenlake?"

"We are," Zoey told her. "I got here yesterday. Pete has been here for about three days."

"That makes sense." Wanda nodded. "I've sensed magic in the air...powerful magic...enough to tear open the fabric of the universe." She paused. "Tell me, are you from a different world?"

"You're perceptive," Pete told her.

Zoey giggled. "Very perceptive. We're from a world called Earth."

"Pete and Zoey from a world called Earth are now in a town called Greenlake, in a country called Lake, in the world of Round." Wanda nodded her head with amusement. "That sounds marvelous." She stopped next to a shelf, reaching for a box on it. "Oh, here we are."

With slow care, using two hands, she slid the box from the shelf. Then she held under it with one hand, lifting the lid as she rotated to show Zoey. It was a black band. On its exterior, a thread of gold formed the images of a sun and a moon. "Here you go, deary. This is what you search for."

"It's beautiful," Zoey admired it, taking the box from her. "What does it do?"

Wanda smiled. "It's called the Ring of Day Walking. It is one of a kind. For most people, it doesn't do anything. For you, it will. You might not have noticed it. The sun causes a gradual drain to a vampire's HP. Also, the sun hurts their eyes. This ring will grant you immunity to the sun. Wear it, and the sun won't hurt your eyes; it won't drain your HP."

"I noticed the eye part," Zoey confirmed.

"Good, deary, so you understand how valuable this is. It is a bit pricy, though." Wanda explained. "It'll cost you 300 len."

"300 len?" Pete's jaw dropped. 300 len was a lot for a single ring, but if it protected Zoey, it would be worth the price.

Zoey hung her head, "That is a lot. I only have 100…"

"We'll take it." Pete cut in.

"No, you can't." Zoey protested.

"I insist." He smiled at her.

"Thank you," She hugged him.

He blushed, not used to hugs, but he managed to squeak out. "You're welcome."

"See," Wanda said. "You are like a couple."

"We are not." Zoey and Pete said in unison.

After making the purchase, Pete and Zoey went back to Mod's to return the cloak. With the new ring for Zoey, she no longer had to hide from the sun. Their next stop was back at the smith to pick up the metal components of their uniforms. Their next stop would be Tay the leatherworker and seamstress.

As they walked, Zoey asked, "Do they have a place to get cell phone service here?"

"I looked yesterday morning," Pete explained. "I didn't find anything. Mod said we'd have to go to the next town over to find a provider. He said the provider has accessories and stuff. Once we get the pixie's ready to run a few shifts without us, we'll be able to take a few days off and go."

"Cool," she gave the thumbs up as they arrived at Tay's.

They walked in to see Tay. She was entering from the backdoor, wearing a worn apron, her hair tied back, thick gloves up to the elbows. Pete guessed she was boiling leather in a backroom or behind the store.

"Ah," the elvan seamstress grinned upon seeing Pete. "It's good to see you again. Did you change your mind about that date?"

"Uh…" Pete's mind went blank. How was he even supposed to respond to that? Why did Tay have to say that in front of Zoey? "I…uh…we have a job for you."

"We?" Tay scanned her eyes over to Zoey, and her grin faded. "Who is we?"

"This is Zoey." Pete squeaked out.

Before Pete could introduce Tay to Zoey, Zoey spoke. As Pete looked at Zoey, he could swear her eyes had gone from green to red. Was that a vampire trait, or did he imagine things? She said. "Hi. I'm Pete's roommate and best friend. My name is Zoey."

"Roommate?" Tay glowered.

"And best friend." Zoey wrapped her arm around Pete, "We go everywhere together."

"I see. How unfortunate." Tay frowned. After a few seconds, she pushed away from her jealousy and forced a smile. "And what brings you both in today? How can I help you?"

Zoey removed her arm from Pete's shoulder and stepped closer, explaining. "We need some uniforms for ourselves and our co-workers at Mod's Pizzeria." Zoey turned back to Pete. "Pete, show her the designs."

Pete broke from his mental stupor. "Right, designs…here they are." He materialized the designs, walked over to Tay, and began to show her."

"I can make these." She confirmed. "But I'll need the metal pieces. I can't do any of the smithing."

"We have those right here." Pete materialized them and placed them on the table that Tay used for sewing. "How much will it cost? We have 50 squares of high-quality leather that we can provide. Anything left over is open for trade. Or we can pay in len."

Even though Mod gave Pete len to pay for the uniforms, Pete hoped Tay would accept leather squares as payment. After all, Pete and Zoey had the most expensive uniforms, and they'd be using them outside the store. It didn't seem fair to make Mod pay for all of it.

"Forty squares," Tay answered. "That will cover the cost of making the uniforms as well as provide me the materials I need for these designs."

"Sounds great," Zoey said. "Any idea how long it will be?"

"Give me two hours." Tay requested.

"Two hours it is," Zoey replied, turning to Pete and winking. "That will give Pete and me plenty of time to finish our date."

Pete blushed again.

Tay went back to frowning.

By 1:00 PM, Zoey and Pete returned to the pizzeria, new uniforms in hand. By the time the pixies arrived, Zoey, Pete, and Mod had changed into the new garb.

When Hope saw it, her eyes widened. "They look amazing! I worked so hard on them, and now they are here. That was so quick. You made them so fast. Thank you so much. This is amazing."

"Here is yours." Pete handed the little pixie her uniform before handing out uniforms to the other pixies. They took turns using Mod and Zoey's room to change. Each of the pixies praised Hope for her creative designs. Then, they began prepping pizza toppings for the afternoon shift.

194

27: Delivery Shift

Zoey began her shift. It was the first shift where she and Pete would take deliveries. It was exciting for her to get out and see the town by herself. It wasn't that she didn't appreciate Pete's company—in fact, she loved having him around—but she also needed some alone time. She wanted to feel the excitement of getting to explore a new place.

She used that time to learn the town's layout as she traversed it time and time again. One of her deliveries took her passed a three-story, yellow building. It was near the Southeast corner of the plaza. It was taller than any she'd seen, so she took the time to get a better look. As she slowed to look at its sign, she learned it was the schoolhouse.

Concrete steps ran up and down parallel to the school's entrance. It allowed people that lived on lower streets or higher ones to reach the front door. A fence jutted out from the wall's southern corners, creating a square of chain-link fence. The metal fence surrounded a playground with swings, slides, and monkey bars.

She appreciated how similar the playground was to the ones they had back on Earth. As she thought about it, she let a smile creep across her face. Then she hurried toward her delivery.

Taking a delivery for M&P's in Greenlake was a different experience than taking one back on Earth. She contrasted the difference in her mind.

Instead of having a car, Zoey had to walk the deliveries to their respective destinations. If she had to carry them in a physical sense, balancing pizzas while walking for blocks.

What would have made things more complicated was how M&P's didn't have boxes for the pizza yet. Instead, Mod was transferring the cooked pizza from a hot baking screen to a cool one. The Driver would lift the screen and dematerialize it into their inventory. When they arrived at the address, they'd rematerialize it. Zoey wished she could have done that with her deliveries back on Earth. It made things so much easier.

Another thing that made things easier was how she only had to think about the house where she had to deliver. When she did, a waypoint arrow appeared in her mini-map; she didn't have to worry about getting lost.

Without having to hold anything in her hands and without having to worry about navigation, she sprinted to the address. Then she ran back to the pizzeria. She repeated it again. Then she did it again.

At some point, she realized that where she could run without getting tired, Pete wasn't able to. It helped her take triple the deliveries he could. She wondered if her unlimited stamina came from her being a vampire. She guessed it did.

How did she become a vampire? She wondered. Why wasn't Pete one? She had a theory about it.

Pete said he fell from the tree when he saved the cat; she had not. The last thing she remembered before waking up in Pizza and Games was the girl with Max the Cat. That woman in the nightgown had a creepy aura, and the last thing Zoey remembered was seeing that woman's teeth.

If I had fallen when Max lunged at me, Zoey realized, *Max would have brought me to this world as a human.* If Pete hadn't fallen, would he be a vampire? Zoey wondered if she'd ever see that other woman or max, again.

"Watch out, lady!" A child's voice shouted toward Zoey as she sprinted toward one of her deliveries.

She turned in the direction of the voice to see a red ball zipping toward her head. As she focused on it, it began to slow like how the air hockey puck had slowed when she played the game against Max.

It gave her enough time to lift her hands and catch the ball in stride like a wide receiver running a slant pattern. After making the catch, she slowed to a jog and focused on the kids. There were three, two boys and a girl. She hurled the ball back to the girl who caught it and shouted, "thanks."

"Anytime," Zoey yelled back. Then she continued toward her delivery.

When Zoey gained some distance from the kids, she heard one of the boys say. "That was awesome. She had the reflexes of a ninja."

A ninja or a vampire, Zoey thought.

She still wasn't sure what it meant to be a vampire. Part of her wished she had asked Wanda more questions about vampires in Round. The other part of her was afraid to know about them.

Was it only a matter of time before she converted into some blood-sucking fiend? Or would she keep receiving sustenance from regular food? She should figure those things out sooner rather than later.

When she arrived at the next house—it was turquoise on the outside with a yellow door, a woman answered the door. She was short with blond hair, a red hat, and a striped white and blue shirt. From what Zoey could tell, she was a gnome.

"Hi," Zoey smiled. "I have an order for Yam Hopler."

"That's me," Yam answered back, her eyes squinting to get a better look at Zoey. "I don't know you. Are you new to town? I thought I knew everyone in town. First, we have Pete that is new here. Now, we have you that are new here." Yam blinked a few times and leaned back, recomposing. "I'm sorry about that. What I mean to say is hello. My name is Yam Hopler—I guess you already knew that—and I am the mayor of Greenlake. It's nice to meet you."

"Nice to meet you, too," Zoey giggled, materializing the pizza and giving it to the mayor. As the mayor took it, len appeared in Zoey's inventory. "We will have to talk later. I have more people waiting for their dinner."

"I'm looking forward to it." The Mayor answered. "Have a great night."

"You, too." Zoey began to jog away. "Have a good one." Zoey heard the door close, and she continued back to the store.

She took three more deliveries before her delivery shift ended, and M&P's closed for the night.

As Mod closed the doors, he turned to the pixies, to Pete, and to Zoey. "Tonight was busy. In all my life, I don't know if I've ever worked so hard. And you all kept up. I can't thank you all enough.

"With this, I have some good news for everyone. After collecting the payment for all the orders, I've realized how much we made today. In three days of serving pizza in the bakery, we've earned what used to take me a full month.

"To thank you all, I want to double your pay." He smiled. "You've all earned it."

The pixies cheered, doing their signature celebrations. The only difference was this time Skye did a quadruple dab back and forth.

As the pixies and Mod said goodnight to each other and to Pete and Zoey. Pete and Zoey did the same back. Then the pixies returned to their homes, and Mod retreated to his room.

Pete was about to do the same when Zoey turned to him, "Hey, Pete."

"What's up?" Pete asked.

"Before we turn in for the night," Zoey explained. "I was hoping you could go to the forest with me. I want to try to get some experience."

Pete considered her request. "Zoey, I don't think we can go and level up like that. It goes against the laws of the moderators."

"I know, but I have a way around that." She said, following up her declaration with a question. "As a paladin, it is my job to protect people, right?"

"Right," Pete nodded. "That would be my guess.

"So hear me out," Zoey held up a finger, pointing it near his chest. "If you go in search of ingredients for your pizza, and I'm protecting you…"

"That means you'll be doing your job." Pete finished her sentence.

"Bingo," She winked. "We have a winner."

"And what are you going to use for a weapon?" he asked her.

She smiled, causing a pizza peel and pizza fork to materialize in her hands.

Josh Walker

28: Experience Troubles

Without the tomato monsters from the spawn points, Pete didn't know if they could find any of the plant anomalies in the forest. If there were no monsters, they wouldn't be able to level up. Also, he remembered the warnings of Nick Warman about thieves. Plus, it was night. In the dark, without a light, he didn't think he'd be able to see anything.

Still, Zoey pleaded for him to go. "After all," She had said, "I'm a vampire. Night is my jam." Then she went on to explain how seeing in the dark had become easy for her, assuring, "nothing can sneak up on us."

In the end, she convinced him to go with her. As they left the store, he asked her, "Where did you get that peel and fork? Also, why did you choose a peel and fork as your weapons?"

"Well," she began. "You know how you get proficiency bonuses for the pizza fork, peel, cutter, and slapping?"

"Yeah," he confirmed, shoving his hands in his pockets as a cool breeze came up from the lake, causing him to shiver.

"Well, I realized the pizza peel looks like a shield. Then I thought, 'what if it were a shield?' Then I decided to see if the smith would make me a shield that could double as a pizza peel." she held out the peel for him, and he took it.

As he turned it over in his hands, he realized it was thicker than the peel they had in the store. The smith made it from a heavier metal, too. Where the handle on the store peel was stuck in place, the grip on her peel had a small, round release button. It was on the side near where the handle met the flat surface of the peel.

When he pressed the button, the handle folded back behind the peel. This transformed the peel into a legitimate shield.

She explained. "This way, when I get peel proficiency bonuses for working in the store, I'll also get bonuses toward using my shield...er...my peel that is a shield. For the same reason, I chose a pizza fork as a weapon."

"That's smart." The ingenuity impressed him. Still, he wondered. "When did you have time to get these?"

"Between deliveries," she confessed. "Toward the beginning of the shift, I went to the carpenter to have the handle for the fork made. On a delivery after that, I took the handle to the smith and had him finish creating the fork...and I had him make the peel. At the end of the shift, I picked them up on the way back to the store.

"It cost me every len I had, but now I have a weapon and shield. That's something every paladin needs."

"Why didn't you use the store's peel and fork?" He asked.

She wrinkled her nose with disgust. "That isn't sanitary. Can you imagine getting the shield all dirty with tomato monster blood and then using it to pull actual pizzas from the oven?"

"Wouldn't tomato monster blood be ketchup?" He inquired.

"Even so," she said. "It's blah and gross."

"Fair enough," he smiled, looking at her. At that point, he noticed something. "Zoey, I don't mean to change the subject, but your eyes are glowing."

"Glowing?" She asked. "Is this some weird pick up line?"

"No," he assured. "I mean, your eyes, in a literal sense, are glowing in the dark. It is like how crocodile eyes glow at night. If I remember right, they do that because there is something in the eye that reflects light. It makes it easier for them to see at night."

"Did you say I have crocodile eyes?" She flicked the bill of his hat, but after considering her words, she added. "I guess that would make sense. It is weird to be able to see at night. It seems clear as day. Last night, it was like this too, but I figured it was some magic light in the room thing. I didn't realize it was me."

"Well," he readjusted the hat on his head. "As I see it, it's cool. I wish I could see at night."

At this point, the pair reached the outskirts of town and continued toward the mountain.

*　　*　　*

Ragoon the raider watched the city gate, hoping some helpless sap might venture into the countryside. Instead of one sap, he got two, a man and a woman. By the looks of them, they were human. Then he saw their names and levels: Pete LVL 7 and Zoey LVL 1.

He couldn't believe it. The second he saw them, he ran back to the Trash Panda hideout. When he reached it, he hurried through the tunnels and arrived winded to Rumpke's throne room.

Rumpke saw the raider and frowned, "Ragoon, what are you doing here? Aren't you supposed to be at the city gate, mugging anyone dumb enough to leave the safety of the town?"

"Pete the Pizzaman and Zoey...the level one human girl..." Ragoon panted. "...I saw them leave town."

"They left town?" Rumpke smiled. "Which means they will have to go back to town?"

"Right," Ragoon told him. "I know we'd planned to wait until we caught her alone, but with all of us, we can ambush them on the outskirts of town. While some of the raiders keep Pete busy, the others can kidnap the girl."

Rumpke nodded. "Then we can trade her to get back Cedric."

"Exactly," Ragoon agreed.

After some thought, Rumpke began. "I want you to gather everyone on duty, everyone in the tunnels, any able-bodied raccoon you can find."

"As you command," Ragoon saluted.

"Move fast and get the raccoons to the city gate," Rumpke ordered. "We don't know how long Pete and Zoey will be out of town for. If we want to ambush them, we need to be at the gate before they return."

"What about you, my lord?" Ragoon asked.

Rumpke smiled, looking to where he had mounted swords and axes on the wall. "I need to prepare for the confrontation. After I am armed, I will meet you at the gate."

*   *   *

As they reached the boundaries of the town, Zoey pointed into the darkness. "I see someone; it looks like one of those raccoons like the one that tried to rob us the other night."

Pete looked in the direction, but his vision couldn't pierce the darkness. He asked, "what is it doing?"

"It looks like it's running away." She told him, "going toward the forest."

"Chances are that it saw us," Pete told her. "Are you sure you have to do this tonight? I wouldn't want to run into it and its friends."

"I can see it easy enough," Zoey assured. "Nothing will sneak up on us. I promise."

"I trust you," Pete told her, and they continued until they reached the forest. As they began up the mountain path, Pete advised. "We should stay quiet from here. If you have to talk, whisper. We don't want to draw any attention."

"Understood," she told him, asking. "Anything I should look for?"

"Let me know if you see anything. To clarify, I mean things that drop things we can use on pizza. The tomato plant monsters would be perfect. They're called nightshade terrors."

"How did you find them before?" She questioned.

"Before," he told her. "I had Nick the guard and waypoint arrows. It was part of some quests. Since the plants I hunted won't respawn for another four days or so, we're on our own."

"That's lame," she sighed. "But we've got to do what we've got to do. Let's go."

They pushed beyond the tree line and up the mountainside. Pete found the forest-covered mountains to be different at night. Instead of a breeze warming his face, the cold night wind rattled the branches and rustled leaves.

As he tried to listen for sounds, all he could hear was, woosh, woosh, woosh, wooooosh. If a nearby animal moved a bush, he wouldn't be able to tell it apart from the wind. This coupled with the fact that he couldn't see, making him feel defenseless.

The last time he felt that way was as a seven-year-old child. He'd watched a scary movie before bed, and a nightmare woke him. It was midnight, and he was alone in a dark room. All he could do was call for his mom and dad to save him.

This time, there was no one to save him. After all, Zoey was only level one. If worse came to worst, Pete would be the one who had to defend them. To prepare for that, he kept his senses on edge, ready to react at the first sign of danger.

"Don't be so jumpy." She reprimanded with a whisper. "I promise I can see fine. Trust me. I'll tell you if anything is around."

"Do you think Wanda has any items for night vision?" He whispered back. "If she does, night leveling will be so much easier."

"Yeah," she let the first word hang before continuing. "But that wouldn't be near as fun for me."

"You're evil." He told her.

She thought about what he said and replied. "My status page says I'm chaotic good. That makes you wrong on an objective level."

"The status page is wrong." He teased. "It hasn't known you for as long as I have."

In response, she stuck her tongue out at him. Of course, he didn't see it, not with how dark it had gotten.

A branch cracked under his foot, and she laughed. "This is so fun and creepy. It's like that haunted house downtown that they put on every year for Halloween. I love it."

"You're a vampire," he replied. "You would love it."

"Hold on," she grabbed him by the shoulder, holding him in place. "There is something up ahead. Nightshade terror mutant. It's level six."

"Huh," he'd never heard of a mutant monster before. He wondered what made it different from a normal one. If it made it stronger than usual, it could give him a hard time. "How big is it? Are there any other monsters with it?"

"A little taller than you, and no," she shook her head. "I only see the one."

He realized the growth from level three to level six didn't increase their size as much as it had at lower levels. "Okay, point me in its direction. I'm level seven. I know you're the paladin, but let me tank this one. When you get a few more levels, and when you're level is more even with the monster, you can tank."

"Deal," she said: stepping behind him, taking

him by the shoulders, and pointing him in the direction of the monster. "If you go straight, you'll walk right into it."

"I can't see anything," he explained. "So I'm going to raise my hand. Yell slap when I need to slap. Let's hope that I can kill it in one shot."

"Good luck," she told him.

As soon as he began walking, the battle display appeared in his vision. It showed Zoey's name under his to indicate she was a party member.

He moved slow, careful to feel for branches with his hands and feet. One hit against his shin, but he was moving with enough caution that it would only leave a small bruise. His right foot stepped over it, then his left. And he continued in the same direction, arm raised and ready to strike.

He activated steel hands. Two steps later, he heard his friend's voice, "Slap!"

The palm of his right hand swung at around where he guessed the head would be. Instead, he hit across the shoulder. He could feel the monster resist the blow. But only at first. Then he swung through with ease, lifting it.

He heard leaves rustle as it fell; then came a dull thump. Had it hit a tree stump? That was his best guess. Yet, he had a more important question. Was it dead? If not, he wouldn't be able to fight one of these things in the dark. A prompt appeared, putting his mind at ease:

You defeated the nightshade terror mutant. You gained 79 experience points.

You received 4 mutant tomatoes
You gained 2 slapping proficiency.

Each shift gave him considerable slapping proficiency, too. He was proud of how much the skill had grown. Even so, he was sad that the monster only offered 79 experience. It wouldn't be enough for Zoey to gain a level.

He returned to her, and they continued to search the forest. After four hours without seeing anything else, they realized the effort was futile.

"I don't get it," He told his friend.

"Don't get what?" She asked.

"What does Max expect us to do? Aside from some plants that respawn weekly, there is no way for us to level up. He wants us to get stronger, but I don't see any way we can do it." He hung his head. "How can we be the heroes of this world?"

"To be honest, this is kinda cool." She told him.

"Yeah?"

"Yeah," she flicked his hat's bill. "To have fun, we used to immerse ourselves in fake worlds. Now we get to live in one of those worlds. But now it is real. Don't be so hard on yourself. In time, we'll figure out how to get stronger. And one of these days, I'll gain a level."

"One of these days." He agreed, fixing his hat.

"But it won't be today." She patted his shoulder. "We should head back and get some sleep."

They made their way back down the mountain path, to the field outside of town. Then they began toward Greenlake's entrance. They hadn't moved more than four paces from the tree line when she stopped him. "Wait, I see some people down there. It looks like the raccoons. Do you think they are waiting for us?"

A strange, deep voice spoke from behind them, "They are waiting for you." At the same time, Pete felt something poke in his back. "My friends down there want to have a chat with you."

In the moonlight, Pete tried to turn his head and locate the source of the voice, but there was no one there. Then he looked at Zoey. Her eyes were wide, her back arched like she also had someone holding a point to it. Pete couldn't see the person behind her, either. Confusion grew on his face.

"What? Ain't you ever seen an invisible raccoon before?" The voice asked.

See an invisible raccoon? Pete knew it was impossible to see an invisible anything. Yet, he didn't want to tell that to someone with a knife pointed at his back. Instead, Pete said. "Okay, let's go talk to your friends."

29: Boss Fight

Pete and Zoey neared the larger group of raccoons, and the lights from the town illuminated the bandits. As soon as he could see them, Pete began to count them. From what he could tell, there were at least fifteen. With the invisible ones behind him and Zoey, that made seventeen.

He wondered how they were invisible, guessing it was some cloak or item. Then again, it was possible that all the raccoons in Round could turn invisible.

From what he could tell, the levels of the raccoons ranged from level five to level thirteen. Most of them carried polearms. The only exception to this was a level twenty named Rumpke.

The level twenty wore a harness with a bronze battle skirt, a thick leather utility belt over the skirt. Rippling muscles covered the creature's frame. He looked like He-Man...if He-Man was a four-foot-tall raccoon.

On the utility belt, Pete saw two knives strapped near the front. A pair of nunchakus hung on the right hip, a short sword on the left. A longer sword strapped at an angle on Rumpke's back, a battleax crossed the other way to form an X.

As they drew near, Rumpke began to speak. "At last, we meet, Pete the pizzaman." The level twenty raccoon opened the fingers on his right hand, protracting pointed claws on each of his five fingers. He drew the claw on his thumb against the one on his pointer finger, creating an unnerving, grinding sound.

"Uh..." Pete stammered, unsure how to answer as he came to a stop before Rumpke. "Meet at last...right...ummm...did you need something? Can I help you?"

Rumpke retracted his claws, examining Pete's face before saying. "Help me?" Then Rumpke laughed.

"Help me, he says. He wonders if he can help me."

The other raccoons began to laugh, their laughter growing with each second until Rumpke held up a finger. The instant he did so, the laughter stopped.

"What do you want?" Zoey asked.

Rumpke's eyes shifted over to Zoey. "I'm glad you asked, dear." Rumpke opened his mouth, using a claw as a toothpick before continuing. "What I want is my brother back."

"Your brother?" Pete sought clarification.

Rumpke hung his head, explaining. "He's a clumsy one, always scheming but never succeeding. The other night, he went to rob you, and now he's in the town's jail."

Pete's heartbeat faster, a wave of understanding slamming into him harder than a Mike Tyson punch. Pete told the raccoon leader. "We don't have your brother. I don't even know where the jail is. I'm not sure how we can help you. What do you want us to do?"

"What do I want you to do? Let me tell you how this is going to work. I'm taking your friend here." Rumpke nodded at Zoey. "Go tell the mayor I'm willing to make a trade. Your friend for my brother."

Pete's stomach clenched. He couldn't let Zoey get kidnapped; he had to do something. But what happened if he fought back, and she got hurt? He couldn't risk that. The best play—Pete felt—was to make the trade. He didn't see any other way around it.

"Yeah," Zoey spoke. "I'm not going with anyone."

Rumpke winked at her. "Sorry to say it, my dear, but you don't have a choice." He signaled to his guards. "Take her."

"Nope," Zoey said, spinning and materializing her pizza fork in her right hand, her peel in her left. The peel was already in its shield mode in front of her.

As the armaments appeared, she was mid-spin, arcing the fork across the invisible raccoon behind her.

Though Pete couldn't see it, he heard the dull crack as the fork connected; the injured raccoon whimpered on the ground.

At that moment, Pete's battle prompts activated, and he decided it was time to act. So he spun and slapped three times toward his own invisible foe. He used slap'm silly because he didn't want to kill any of the raccoons.

Two of the three slaps connected, and he received a prompt:

You defeated raccoon raider. You received 320 experience.

Zoey gained two levels.

You received plus 3.1 slapping proficiency.

With the two invisible raccoons taken care of, Pete and Zoey spun to face the others. Knowing the raccoons outnumbered them, Pete doubted their chances. Even so, there was no going back.

He slapped left and right, using slap'm silly. He supplemented attacks with machine gun slap, the skill he'd learned from the Turkey Titan's fingerless glove drop. His agility attribute allowed him to avoid the rusty spear tips of the raccoons.

Zoey ducked, danced, and deflected. She'd parry to the right, block to the left, and swing and fell whenever openings presented.

All the while, the proficiency bonuses, experience, and levels climbed. Pete and Zoey grew more powerful with each defeated enemy.

As strong as they fought, they still took some damage. A glancing blow from a level twelve raider left

Pete with a deep wound across his cheek. Though, he couldn't single out when it happened. Everything was chaotic, disjointed, savage.

Pete had a considerable attack brought about from his high slapping proficiency. Even so, he caught glances of Zoey. He realized she seemed to surpass him in every area.

They couldn't touch her. One spear swung at her head, and she ducked, sliding, avoiding the point by inches. She returned to her feet as she reached her opponent, using the force of her slide to build momentum and bash them with the flat of her shield. It stunned them. Then she wacked them with the wooden dowel part of her fork.

Another charged her, and she stepped to the side, letting it trip over her foot as it overshot. Where she seemed to dominate, she, like Pete, was careful not to kill any of them.

As the raccoon's numbers dwindled, the injured procyonids retreated. Some hid behind Rumpke. Others ran back to the forest. Rumpke growled, shouting at those who fled. "You're going to have toilet cleaning duty for a year!"

Pete's confidence with the situation continued to grow until he felt a stinging pain in his side. He looked down, but he couldn't see what harmed him, no opponent, no weapon. Even so, something had punctured his leather and padded armor. An open wound bled out...and it stung. Even worse, his HP bar had dipped to three-quarters full.

Then he realized. *It's another one of the invisible raccoons.* Panic gripped him. How could he fight something which he couldn't see? In desperation, he slapped in that direction. The only thing he caught was air.

A sharp pain pierced his other side, his HP dipped another full quarter, and he fell to a knee. Realizing he couldn't see his enemy, he became still. It hurt to move, but that wasn't why he became still. Rather, he wanted to listen, hear the next attack coming.

"Pete," Zoey warned, still occupied with two of her own enemies. "To your left, now."

Pete activated slap'm silly and steel hands, then he swung with all his might. His palm landed solid against the face of his invisible enemy. Even though he couldn't see his attacker, he saw dust puff up on the ground where the raccoon fell. A prompt appeared:

You defeated raccoon raider. You received 290 experience.

Congratulations! You gained a level.

Along with the level increase, Pete regained all his HP. The wounds in his side disappeared along with the pain sensation. "Thanks," he shouted to Zoey, wondering how she knew where the enemy was. He'd have to ask her later. He hoped her answer wouldn't be that she smelled Pete's blood on the enemy's weapon or something like that.

While Pete returned to his feet, Zoey finished off the remainder of the raccoon raiders. With the underlings defeated, Pete and Zoey turned to face Rumpke.

The raccoon warlord stood alone, now. Regardless, he was as intimidating as ever. If not for the muscles, the level twenty indicator next to his name was an objective reminder of his strength...even if he was only four feet tall.

During the battle with the other raccoons, Pete had gained four levels. He knew Zoey had gained at least that, but at best, she had raised to level seven. A level seven and a level eleven versus a level twenty. For all intents and purposes, it was a boss fight.

Before they clashed, Rumpke spoke, looking Zoey over, trying to understand how she was so strong. "I've never seen a level one with that kind of power, not a human, anyway. What are you?"

"I'm a vampire." She admitted.

"That makes sense." Rumpke nodded, pulling the two knives from his belt. "It won't save you, though."

In a flash, Rumpke was on them, swinging the blades at Zoey in an unrelenting storm. The pattern of it reminded Pete of the time he'd watched people doing Arnis drills. Right-hand swipe, left-hand swipe, left-hand reverse swipe, right-hand reverse. Then it would repeat. Right, left, left, right. Again...and again...and again...

Zoey contested the blows, using her shield and her polearm, but Pete noticed the panic on her face. She wouldn't be able to keep up with the attacks forever, and Rumpke didn't seem like he would let up any time soon.

Pete used the opportunity to run behind Rumpke, slapping him from behind. Rumpke ducked away from it without breaking rhythm, still unleashing his deadly volley against Zoey.

Pete swung again.

This time Rumpke countered, bringing his shoulder up to deflect the slap. Then the warlord spun in a full circle, catching Pete across the face with an elbow. It opened a cut under Pete's left eye and sent him rolling to the side.

Even so, Zoey took advantage of the break in Rumpke's movements. She used the pronged end of her fork to catch one of the knives and twist, prying the weapon from Rumpke's hand and sending it through the air.

As it landed against the soft grass of the field, Zoey used the back of her fork to knock the second knife away from Rumpke. She lifted her foot and kicked him in the chest.

The attack didn't cause much damage, but it knocked the raccoon off balance. The small mammal rolled backward, returning to his feet. Somewhere during his roll, he had removed the battleax from his back.

Rumpke uses Earthshatter. You received 112 damage.

Rumpke didn't give Zoey time to recover; he ran toward her, ax overhead, ready to finish her off. Pete rolled forward, returning to his feet in a run and activating machine gun slap.

The shockwave of Pete's attack knocked Rumpke to the side, and his grip on the ax loosened. Pete took the chance to slap the broad side of the weapon, tearing it from Rumpke:

You used Machine Gun Slap. You caused 115 damage.

An unarmed, off-balance Rumpke's momentum carried him toward Zoey.

She lifted both of her feet and kicked him straight in the gut:

Zoey attacked Rumpke. Zoey caused 315 damage.

Rumpke let out an UUUFFF as he continued beyond Zoey, falling to the ground. There he rolled another three times, his arms over his stomach.

Though, he didn't stay like that for long, standing as he coughed twice and reach for the nunchakus. Like Michelangelo, Rumpke began to spin the weapon. Twisting it over this shoulder, going from a figure-eight pattern to an inverted version of it, switching the weapon from hand to hand.

Instead of trying to do something fancy like intercept or deflect the weapon, Zoey punched it—and

Rumpke—with the flat of her peel. The attack knocked the weapon—and Rumpke—to the ground:

Zoey used Peel bash. Rumpke received 100 damage.

Rumpke crawled back with a stumble before finding his footing. As he stood, he pulled the gigantic sword from its sheath on his back. "You two are troublesome." He smiled. "But I must admit. I haven't had this much fun in a long time."

Pete didn't answer with his words. Instead, he used his fire ability, summoning a small ball of flame into his right hand. He could feel it, tangible like a baseball, so he held it like a baseball, aimed at Rumpke's face, and threw.

The small ball of fire found its mark, disarming Rumpke and knocking him to the ground. Rumpke remained there, arms out to each side. Then he spoke, "I give up."

You defeated Rumpke. You received 2,000 experience points.

Congratulations! You gained a level.

30: Epiphany

"**G**ive up?" Zoey bared her fangs and hissed. "You tried to kidnap me."

"I wanted my brother back. That was all I wanted." Rumpke answered. His voice seemed somber…sincere. Pete almost felt bad for him.

"Your brother attacked me," Pete explained. "So did you."

Rumpke sat up, legs bent in front of him, and hugged his knees. "The Trash Pandas have to steal. It's one of the laws of the moderators. You must fulfill your calling. If someone tries to do something else or ignores their calling…well… The moderators have destroyed cities for less."

Pete remembered when the mayor indicated that was the punishment for breaking a law of the moderators. He liked the moderators less and less by the second.

Zoey asked. "Your brother stole from us because he has to steal? Your gang steals because stealing is their job? You don't have a choice?"

"The technical term is raiding." Rumpke shrugged. "And no, we don't have a choice. Cedric—my brother—had to steal from you. Then you captured him. I always told mom and dad I'd take care of him…doesn't look like that's going to happen."

"Don't be so hard on yourself." Pete plopped down next to Rumpke, patting Rumpke's shoulder. "You did what you could. What would you say if I told you I have a way to get your brother back?"

Caution entered Rumpke's voice. "You'd help me? Why?"

"Because," Zoey said. "Pete always believes in giving people a second chance. He's always been this way. There was this one time at Pizza Place where a customer didn't tip him four deliveries in a row. Pete was still nice to the customer. It was crazy."

Rumpke blinked. "I don't know what that means."

"It means," Pete explained, "that I have a plan. It will help you and your gang…at the same time…It will help the town of Greenlake."

"I'm listening." Rumpke looked at Pete. "But if you're messing with me, round two of our fight is about to start."

One round against Rumpke was enough. Pete shivered at the thought of round two. Then he hurried to explain. "I overheard the mayor say she needs a garbage man.

"What do you think about being a gang of garbage men?" Pete asked.

"Wouldn't work," Rumpke wasted no time with his answer. "If we get paid to do work, then the moderators won't consider it doing our job."

"I never said you'd get paid for it." Pete stretched his arms up. "In fact, it only works if you don't. Think of it this way. We make big bins that we use to keep garbage in, but we label those bins with big, capital letters, 'Do Not Steal.' Then your gang members come by and steal it."

"Okay," Rumpke offered a toothy smile. "I like how you think. We sort through the do not steal bin items, keeping what we can use, disposing of the rest." Rumpke's smile faded. "One problem, though."

"What's that?" Pete asked as he returned to his feet and offered Rumpke a hand.

Rumpke took his hand and stood. "We won't be able to survive on other people's trash. I have over thirty raccoons who depend on me."

"That's where the second part of my plan comes in," Pete said, pointing at the forested mountain where the raccoons live. "You can keep the forest safe for travelers. If you perceive any threats, you can either handle them or warn us about them. For that, the mayor can pay you. That way, you are still thieves, but you also have honest jobs."

"That doesn't sound fun at all." Zoey rolled her eyes.

Rumpke laughed at her comment before replying to Pete. "The concept of honest thieves seems like a strange one. Yet, if you can make this proposition a reality, I would be happy to acquiesce." He turned his eyes back to Zoey. "Plus, I'd prefer to say on the good side of every vampire with whom my path crosses. I hear they make great allies."

"Oh, you know we do," Zoey added some extra attitude into her words.

Pete clapped his hands together. "Then it's settled. I'll talk to the mayor first thing in the morning, see if she has the funds and means to support a group of forest protectors who moonlight as garbage thieves."

"If she says no?" Rumpke inquired.

"Let's hope she doesn't." Pete took in a deep breath. "But if she does, we'll have to cross that bridge when we come to it. Regardless, I want to offer you a sign of good faith. Whenever you stop by Mod's bakery—we call it M&P's now—you can count on a free slice of pizza. Consider it a sign of good faith. Also, I'll see if I can talk her into releasing your brother."

"For that, I would be eternally grateful." Rumpke put his hands on his hips. "When and how will I know if the mayor accepts these terms?"

Pete contemplated before answering. "Tomorrow, as the sun sets, meet Zoey and me where the path up the mountain meets the tree line. By then, we'll have an answer for you."

"Good," Rumpke nodded his agreement. "Then, I will see you tomorrow night."

"I look forward to it." Pete offered his hand, and Rumpke returned his. After they shook, Rumpke moved to Zoey to shake her hand, too.

"No," Zoey explained, holding her hand as a fist. "Like this. You tap your knuckles against mine." Rumpke did as commanded. "Boom." Zoey opened her hand as if it exploded. "We call it pounds."

"Boom," Rumpke copied, exploding his own fist. "Yes, I do like that. It is entertaining to me. I bid you both a wonderful evening. I will see you tomorrow as the sun sets."

"See you tomorrow," they said in unison, turned, and began toward the town.

As they entered the town, Pete looked at her. "Rumpke mentioned how vampires are stronger than humans. It made me curious. What are your stats like?"

"You don't ask a girl her stats like that." Zoey lectured. "It's like asking them their age."

Was it like asking them their age? Pete hadn't heard that. Did Zoey learn the rule from one of the customers during her delivery shift? Had Pete breached etiquette? His lawful good conscience sank.

"Relax," she giggled. "I was only joking. If I remember, at level one, my strength was thirty-one. Does that help?"

"What?" Pete's heart dropped. "Thirty-one? At level one? When I was level one, my strength was four." Pete pulled up his status screen. "I'm level twelve. My strength is Thirty-seven. What level are you now? What are your stats like?"

"I don't know," she wrinkled her forehead. "Pull up yours, and I'll pull up mine. Let's compare."

They each stopped walking, pulled up their respective status pages, and compared:

NAME: Pete **RACE:** Human **JOB:** Pizzaman

LEVEL 12

HP: 276/276
MP: 21/21

ALIGNMENT: Lawful Good
RELIGION: Christian
LANGUAGES: English, Spanish, Common

STR: 37
DEX: 27
VIT: 29
INT: 21
SPR: 16
AGI: 26

GENDER: Male
HEIGHT: 5'8
WEIGHT: 145 lbs
AGE: 20
EYES: Blue
Hair: Blond

LEFT ARM: Unequipped
RIGHT ARM: Unequipped
HEAD: M&P Combat Hat
BODY: M&P Battle Top
LEGS: M&P Battle Pants
FEET: Combat Boots
HANDS: Fingerless Titan Gloves
NECKLACE: Unequipped
EARRINGS: Unequipped
Ring 1: Silver Claddagh
Ring 2: Unequipped

ATTACK: 677
DEFENSE: 569
MAGIC ATTACK: 10
MAGIC DEFENSE: 48

PROFICIENCIES: Slapping Skill 101.2, Slapping Defense 10, Tree Climbing -5, Running 27, Tackling 1, Slashing defense 19.3, Light Armor 47.2, Pizza Cutter 17.3, Pizza Peel 7.2, Jumping 7.2, Evasion 21

Experience: 1650/1800

NAME: Zoey **RACE:** Vampire **JOB:** Paladin
(Subjob) Pizzawoman

LEVEL 11

HP: 310/310
MP: 46/46

STR: 42
DEX: 37
VIT: 43
INT: 46
SPR: 32
AGI: 67

ALIGNMENT: Chaotic Good
RELIGION: None
LANGUAGES: English,
Japanese
Common
GENDER: Female
HEIGHT: 5'5
WEIGHT: 110 lbs
AGE: 19
EYES: Black
Hair: Green

LEFT ARM: Combat Pizza Peel
RIGHT ARM: Combat Pizza Fork
HEAD: M&P Combat Hat
BODY: M&P Battle Top
LEGS: M&P Battle Skirt
FEET: Combat Boots
HANDS: Unequipped
NECKLACE: Gold Pendant
EARRINGS: Obsidian Earrings
Ring 1:   Silver Claddagh
Ring 2:   Ring of Day Walking

ATTACK: 3740
DEFENSE: 936
MAGIC ATTACK: 23
MAGIC DEFENSE: 600

PROFICIENCIES: Slapping Skill 6.1, Air Hockey 121.9, Tree Climbing 10, Pizza Cutter 7.1, Pizza Peel 92.3, Evasion 70.2 Pizza Fork 89.7, Light Armor 18.3

Experience: 739/1600

"Wh…wh…what?" He stammered, unable to believe the difference in their attributes. She was tougher in every category. All that because she was a vampire. He understood why Rumpke wanted to remain friends with vampires.

Zoey remained wide-eyed, staring straight ahead as they closed the screens and resumed walking. A sly smile snuck across her lips, and she said. "It's okay to be weak. Not everyone can be strong and awesome."

"Funny…" Pete glowered. "Then again, if you weren't as strong as you are, we wouldn't have defeated those raccoon raiders. I'm glad you're okay."

"Thanks." She put her arm around his shoulder and hugged. "I'm glad you're okay, too."

"Speaking of the battle." Pete tried not to blush as she hugged him. "How did you know where the invisible raccoon was? The one that stabbed me in each side?"

"I smelled your blood on his knife." She grinned, adding. "It smelled tasty…"

"Funny joke." Pete smiled.

"I know. I'm a funny vampire." She released her hold on him.

They came to Mod's bakery, opened the door with an iron key which Mod had given Pete, and entered inside. Both remained as quiet as possible, sneaking back to their room. Once there, Zoey lied in the bed, and Pete claimed his spot atop the hay in the corner.

Before falling asleep, Pete carried out one more task. He opened up his job skills screen and began to allocate the points he'd earned from gaining five levels.

He started by allocating points to strong fire. The standard fire spell had saved them in their fight against Rumpke. It only made sense to further develop the skill.

Next, he put three points into strong steel hands,

knowing it would boost his slapping ability. That would help him in battle and in the kitchen. After unlocking the ability, he had eleven remaining points.

He unlocked strong heat resist next, lowering the total job points remaining to eight. And he had three options to choose from: oven survival, cut resist, and milk to cheese.

Oven survival would grant him the ability to touch hot pans in the oven with his bare hand without getting burned. It could be helpful for loading and removing pizzas.

Yet, Mod tended to the oven during shifts. During work, Pete took deliveries and helped with slapping and topping pizzas. Unless he filled in for Mod, the ability wouldn't help him. It could wait.

Cut resist offered a twenty percent resistance to slashing, stabbing, and cutting damage. It was a no brainer, so he put points into it, lowering his total remaining job points to five.

This unlocked a new ability, pizza cutter accuracy. It added five extra damage points when he had a pizza cutter equipped. Since he hadn't yet fought with a cutter, he chose not to unlock it.

Instead, he scanned his eyes back to milk to cheese. It allowed him to turn a quart of milk into a block of cheese in an instant. He wondered if the ability would save Mod money on cheese. After careful consideration, he unlocked it.

A new trait appeared, a line connecting it to milk to cheese. The new trait was tomato to sauce. It would turn one tomato into a quart of sauce. It was another useful trait, so Pete put two points into it, leaving him with one.

With that, he closed the job skills menu, closed his eyes, and slept.

31: Truce

The late night took a toll on Pete. His worn body needed the rest. By the time he woke up, it was already ten in the morning. Pete looked to Zoey's bed but didn't see her.

He sat up and stretched, lifting his hands over his head. As he did, he realized he was still in his uniform. With everything that had happened, he forgot to change into his pajamas.

In a way, that made waking u easier. He didn't have to worry about getting changed. He rose to his feet and hurried out of the bedroom and into the bakery.

Mod worked making the morning pastries while listening to music and dancing. Zoey sat at one of the dine-in tables, holding a cinnamon role in her right hand. She was mid-bite when she noticed Pete. When she saw him, she hurried to swallow and said. "Good morning, sleepyhead."

"Good morning," Pete answered, scanning from Zoey to Mod then back to Zoey. "I'm going to go see the mayor. Did either of you need anything while I'm out?"

"No," Zoey shook her head.

"I'm good," Mod answered while still dancing.

"Okay, have a nice morning," Pete said.

"You too," Zoey said, taking another bite of her breakfast as Pete sped out the door.

At a jogger's pace, he began toward the Mayor's office, waving to people as he went by them. Lilly the carpenter—Mod's sister—smiled and waved back. Next to her, Tay the leatherworker and seamstress said, "looking good in those clothes. Whoever made them did an excellent job."

"They did," Pete answered as he trotted along.

Next, he encountered Nolan the pixie. When No-

Ian saw Pete, the pixie changed direction, flying parallel with Pete's head, keeping perfect pace. "Tomorrow after work, I have a concert with my band. We're called the Perplexing Pixies. I want to invite you and Zoey to come."

"I'll be there." Pete kept jogging.

Nolan air guitared to celebrate before flying back in the same direction from where he came.

Pete reached the mayor's building, slowing as he went through the front door. Then he sped walked the rest of the way to her office. The office door remained shut, but he could hear voices on the other side.

"I don't know what happened." It was Nick the guard's voice. "There are raccoon footprints everywhere. It looks like there was a fight."

"You said it happened on the outskirts of town?" The mayor asked.

Pete didn't mean to listen in, and he didn't want to interrupt, but he knew what had happened. Since Pete needed to tell the mayor something related to what Nick was telling her, Pete knocked.

"We are having an important discussion," Nick called from the other side. "Go away."

"It's Pete," Pete answered. "I know what happened last night…on the outskirts of town."

For five seconds, Nick did not answer. The Mayor did not respond. Pete didn't say anything else. Silence filled the air. As the door cracked open, it creaked, breaking the silence. Nick peaked through the space between the frame and the door. "Son, you said you know what happened?"

Pete nodded that he did.

"Moderators," Nick opened the door the rest of the way. "You are always in the middle of everything. Didn't I tell you to stay out of trouble? It was one of the first things I said when you came to Greenlake."

"I am," Pete held up his hand. "Scout's honor."

"Son, I don't know what that means." Nick scowled.

"It means I have some good news, and it relates to last night," Pete explained.

Nick squinted his eyes, staring contemplatively at Pete the pizzaman. After a few intense seconds, Nick's expression softened, and he pulled the door the rest of the way open.

Pete stepped inside, Nick shutting the door behind him. As Pete stood in front of the mayor's desk, she asked him, speaking with her nervous, fast speech. "You say you know what happened last night, so I have to ask. We must know. It's been driving me crazy. What happened last night?"

"After we closed M&P's last night, Zoey and I went to the forest. We wanted to see if we could find any stray tomato plants for the pizza sauce at the restaurant." Pete began. "On our way back to town, Rumpke and his gang attacked us."

"Rumpke..." Nick growled at hearing the name.

Pete continued. "We fought off Rumpke's subordinates..."

"By yourselves?" Nick interrupted. Pete shook his head yes. "Son, that is impressive. Good work."

"There's more," Pete explained. "After we defeated the underlings, Rumpke attacked. We beat him, too."

Nick's mouth hung open, but for once, the guard was speechless. Still, Nick's expression demonstrated his thoughts as well as words could. In his mind, he said. You beat Rumpke? Good job, son. Let's celebrate with bacon. Or something like that.

"As it turns out, Rumpke and his raiders only rob because it is their job to rob. They are following the laws of the moderators." Pete paused, knowing the next part was going to be a hard sell. "So I thought they could be your garbage men, but instead of paying them, you let them steal the garbage."

The mayor blinked three times, staring at Pete. "For a long time now, these raccoons have tormented our town. Now, you want me to give them a job?"

"You need a garbage man." Pete reminded her. "The Trash Pandas will do the work for free. You don't even have to pay them. After all, if you did pay them, they wouldn't be stealing. In fact, you can't pay them so that they can obey the laws of the moderators."

"I don't like it." She diverted her eyes downward, thinking. "Even so, it might be my best option."

"There's more," Pete told her. He didn't mean to come off so blunt.

"More?" Nick asked.

"Cedric—the thief who is in jail—is Rumpke's brother. It would mean a lot to Rumpke if you would let his brother go free." Pete tapped his chin. "And there's one other thing."

"Other thing?" Nick and the mayor asked in unison.

"The garbage the Trash Pandas dispose of will provide them with some of the things they need to survive. But it won't give them everything they need. Rumpke has agreed to protect the forest where they live. All he asks is for some pay." As Pete finished, he tried to gauge the reactions of Nick and the mayor.

The only emotion he got from them was disbelief. He couldn't decide if it was happy disbelief or angry disbelief, so Pete decided to add one more thing. "If the raiders attack a monster or an enemy outside of town, it goes along with their raiding and stealing job. They will be able to protect in the forest and on the outskirts of Greenlake."

Nick interrupted, humility entering into his voice. "That will mean they can protect Greenlake's citizens where I can't. Son, first you save the town by inventing an all meat pizza...now you do this. Thank you."

"And Rumpke's agreed to this?" The mayor asked. "No backsies?"

"No backsies," Pete said. "At sunset, I told him I'd let him know what you thought about all of it."

The mayor interlocked her fingers, resting her hands on her desk, and said. "Pete, tonight, when you meet with Rumpke, this is what I want you to do..."

*   *   *

Zoey looked at the endless countryside, amazed at the beauty it offered. The emerald fields contrasted with the orange sky created by the setting sun. At the tree line, atop the muddy path, she and Pete waited for Rumpke.

Pete offered to go by himself, but Zoey wasn't going to allow it. She didn't trust Rumpke like Pete did. It didn't mean she distrusted Rumpke, either. In the end, she knew when dealing with raccoon warlords, it's better to err on the side of caution."

The sunset in full, turning the orange sky to darkness, stars flickering, a moon hidden by the clouds. A short time after, Rumpke emerged from the trees. No sooner had he seen Pete than he ran toward him.

At first, Zoey thought Rumpke would attack Pete, but then she realized that wasn't the case. Rumpke hugged Pete and said. "Thank you. Cedric returned home at noon. He told me everything. I can't believe you did it."

"It was our pleasure to help." Pete patted the shorter man on the back. "It was no trouble. Are you ready to go eat dinner? The mayor is waiting for you at the pizzeria."

"I am ready, Master Pete." Rumpke released the embrace signaling with an open town toward the town. "Lead the way."

Pete did as instructed, taking the lead as they

moved up and down hills, remaining on the muddy pathway.

Zoey remained back with Rumpke, not wanting to turn her back on the small—but muscular—mammal. She asked him. "What are you going to do now? For you, I mean."

Rumpke looked up at her as they walked. "I'm not sure what you mean."

"Your raiders can steal the garbage, so they are still doing their jobs." She explained. "You're a warlord. In a way, you've always waged war on Greenlake. Now, you won't be. How will you fulfill your job?"

"I hadn't thought about it." Rumpke hung his head.

She patted him on the top of the head. "Don't worry. I have an idea."

He looked up at her with a toothy grin. "Is that right?"

"That's right," she nodded, whispering so Pete couldn't hear. "Have you ever heard of a prank?"

"A prank?" He whispered back. "No, that sounds fascinating. Tell me. What's a prank?"

"It's when you do a harmless joke to someone like moving their communication box from the left side of their desk to the right side. One time, I moved my manager's desk an inch closer to the wall every day. He didn't notice until his desk was up against the wall. It was hilarious." She chuckled.

"That does sound entertaining. I'm not sure how that helps me be a warlord, though." He raised a questioning eyebrow.

"Simple," Zoey replied, still whispering. "You declare harmless prank wars on people. They prank you. You prank them back. It would make you a prank warlord."

"A prank warlord." Rumpke laughed. "I like the sound of that."

Pete looked back. "What are you both laughing about?"

"Nothing," Zoey and Rumpke answered at the same time, their laughter growing.

The trio entered the town and continued until they reached the pizzeria. Through the picture frame window, light beamed. It provided a clear view of inside the restaurant.

Every Mod and Pete's Pizzeria and Baked Good's employees was there. The pixies danced in the air while Mod sat with Nick and the mayor at one of the tables. Everyone smiled, talked, and laughed, two pizzas on the table between them. Music sounded loud enough to hear it from outside.

As Rumpke, Pete, and Zoey went inside. The jovial atmosphere turned quiet; someone even turned the music off. Everyone's eyes fixated on Rumpke. Rumpke looked back, scanning over everyone until his eyes met Nick Warman's.

And they stared at each other. In the end, Rumpke broke the silence. "Nick, I hear there is an all meat pizza."

"There is," Nick confirmed.

"Can I please try a slice?" Rumpke walked over to the table sitting between Mod and the mayor. Someone had set a spot for Rumpke there, including a plate.

"You can." Nick agreed, using a spatula to serve an all meat slice to the raccoon.

Rumpke examined the food, and everyone watched as he lifted it to his mouth, bit, and chewed. He was deliberate with his slow movements, but after he tasted the food, a smile crept across his face. He even clapped twice as he exclaimed. "This is excellent."

The pixies did their textbook celebrations as Nick said. "I'm glad you like it. I also want to thank you for agreeing to protect the people in the country and forest. The people of Greenlake mean a lot to me, and it is decent of you to protect them."

"You're welcome," Rumpke answered, gesturing to Nick's plate. "Your plate is empty. Would you like another slice of all meat pizza?"

"I would enjoy that very much." Nick agreed.

This time, Rumpke took the spatula, but instead of serving Nick an all meat slice, Rumpke served a slice of cheese. Nick stared at him. Then Rumpke said. "It's a prank." And Rumpke laughed. Then Nick laughed.

At that moment, the tension in the room broke, and everyone else began to laugh. While the atmosphere was light, Zoey suggested, "Turn the music back on." When a song began to play, she took Pete by the hands. "Let's dance."

Pete let her guide him by the hand to an open space where they began to dance. Pete looked ridiculous, of course. He never was a good dancer. As the song ended, she hugged him and told him. "You've done a lot for this town. Who would have thought that pizza would be the glue that brought it together?"

Pete shrugged. "Everybody loves pizza."

She smiled in agreement, thinking, *everyone loves pizza. Pete the pizzaman more than most.*

Hope's Drawing Board

Front Cover Art: Manuel Aguila
Back Cover Art: Kiit Watson
Interior Illustrations: Kiit Watson, ance.art, Hindy355, Esperanza Walker, and Josh Walker